STRANGER

IN MY HOUSE

A Novel by

Christina Fletcher

Copyright 2019 © Christina Fletcher

Published by Major Key Publishing, LLC

www.majorkeypublishing.com

ALL RIGHTS RESERVED.

Any unauthorized reprint or use of the material is prohibited. No part of this book may be reproduced or transmitted in any form or by any means, electronic, or mechanical, including photocopying, recording, or by any information storage without express permission by the publisher.

This is an original work of fiction. Names, characters, places and incidents are either products of the author's imagination or are used fictitiously and any resemblance to actual persons, living or dead is entirely coincidental.

Contains explicit language & adult themes suitable for ages 16+

About the Author

Christina Fletcher was born and raised in St. Louis, Missouri, where you'll notice most of her stories are based. She has a master's degree in human services and works as a community support specialist with individuals who have intellectual and developmental disabilities. When this married mother of three, and three bonus children, isn't writing, she enjoys taking trips, reading, singing, and fishing. Christina is also working on a project to establish her own nonprofit organization. In the meantime, she looks forward to bringing more new and entertaining stories to her readers.

Dedication

This book is dedicated to those who have been struggling to find themselves in the midst of being there for other people. Now is your time to shine. Take a deep breath, and let go of all that negative energy. Be true to who you are, and don't allow yourself to be blinded by your emotions.

Christina's Catalog

I Can't Trust You: Friends, Lovers & Lies

I Can't Trust You: Friends, Lovers & Lies 2

I Can't Trust You: Friends, Lovers & Lies 3

Nothing is Promised: Vamp & Keyani's Love Story

Loyalty is Everything: Betrayal of Friends & Lovers

Loyalty is Everything: Betrayal of Friends & Lovers 2

Loyalty is Everything: Betrayal of Friends & Lovers 3

Perfect Imperfections: A Tale of Love & Dishonor

Hope For A Misfit

Hope For a Misfit 2

R.E.A.L. (Remember Everybody Ain't Loyal)

Loving You Was Not For Me (Anthology)

Fooled By So-Called Love (Anthology)

Amazon:

http://www.amazon.com/author/christinafletcher.

Facebook:

www.facebook.com/authoresschristinafletcher/

Website: www.authoresschristinafletcher.com

Chapter 1 Almi

"Kane!" I yelled out to my boyfriend as I walked through the door. I set the bags of groceries I was carrying down on the counter. I had two more heavy bags in the car, and I needed for him to help me carry them. "Kaaaaane!"

"Yeah, bae?" he replied, finally popping his head into the kitchen. My heart melted when I saw his sexy face. I loved this man so much, and everything about him turned me on. He had a medium-caramel complexion, a neatly-trimmed goatee, and low haircut he wore with waves. Kane stood about five-ten and had the deepest-brown eyes that were easy to get lost in. This man was my everything, and the amazing part was that I knew he felt the same way about me.

"I have two more bags of groceries in the car," I told him, as I started putting away the ones I brought in.

He blew out a breath and put down the PlayStation 4 controller he was holding. I rolled my eyes, wishing he would find something less childish to do all day. Don't get me wrong, I knew how men were about their video games. Technically, I didn't find anything wrong with him playing; however, what I had an issue with was his being on the game all day versus looking for a job. That is what made me say he was being childish.

"Why do you always use paper bags instead of plastic?" he asked as he came back in and set both bags on the counter.

"I can get more down in them. I would rather just have a couple of bags to carry versus ten," I told him.

"I guess." He shrugged. "That would make sense if you were the one carrying them though. I still say that plastic bags are easier to carry."

"Well then, next time, *you* go to the grocery store so *you* can have the groceries bagged however *you* want," I suggested.

"Yeah, I see that's what I'm gonna have to do," he said, snatching the game controller off the counter and heading back into his man cave.

I shook my head, suddenly growing frustrated. Like I said, I was crazy about this man, but I could not deal with him getting too comfortable about not having a job. I knew all about a woman needing to being strong and holding her man down during times of need, but I didn't have it in me to do this forever. While I believed that should be the case temporarily, it should not be a prolonged case. I am a firm believer that if a man don't work, he don't eat.

Kane was laid off from his job about three months ago, and although he was receiving unemployment benefits, it barely helped to make up for what we were lacking financially. We had to go into our savings to make up the extra loss, and I was sure that would eventually run dry if he didn't find some type of job soon.

I finished putting away the groceries and stood at the sink to fill a glass of water. I downed the first glass, and right as I refilled another, I looked out the kitchen window into the back yard, and frowned. The grass looked like it was damn near knee-high. It took everything in me not to scream and pull my hair out. This shit was driving me insane having to constantly ask Kane to do things around here. Since he was home all the time, the least bit he could do was help maintain our home. It's like he got more and more lazy the longer he was out of work. I was at the point that I was about to sit down, start completing job applications online, and submit whatever resumes I could for him. I shouldn't have to do that when he wasn't even making an effort for himself though.

"Kaaaaane!" I called out to him again. I waited a few seconds and was about to holler out again when he walked back into the kitchen looking annoyed.

"What now?" he asked, scrunching up his face.

"The trash needs to be taken out, and the grass is ridiculously high. Since you're not really doing anything, can you *please* cut it?"

"That sounded like a little shade there, but I'm gonna act like it wasn't. Let me finish up this game, and I got you. What are you cooking for dinner?"

"Really, Kane? I've been at work all day and had to make a grocery-store run. I'm tired. Can't you cook dinner?"

"You want me to handle the front and backyard don't you? I'll be tired when I finish that."

"Fine, just… Oh my God!" I yelled out, and threw my head back, unable to even finish my thought. "Just order from Door Dash tonight. I'm going to go take a shower."

"What do you have a taste for?"

"Surprise me."

"Em, em. Nope. I'm not falling for that one. You're always indecisive, and whenever I pick something, it's never right. So I'm gonna ask you again. What do you have a taste for?"

"I said *surprise* me." I rolled my eyes, and walked away.

"Taco Bell?" he called out.

"Anything but Taco Bell!" I yelled back to him.

"See what I mean? I can't win for losing!"

I laughed because he was right. I definitely didn't want that dog food Taco Bell served. Yuck. I wish they had never closed down Del Taco because their food was the shit. Now if he would have said Qdoba or Chipotle, I would have been game. Hell, he could have even said Fuzzy Taco, but I'm not sure if they were setup on Door Dash yet.

I got in the shower, and the hot water felt good cascading down my body. I thought about when Kane and

I met in college. We were both students at Maryville University here in St. Louis, Missouri. I'm originally from St. Louis and didn't want to leave for school, so I stayed to attend college locally. Kane came here from Kansas City, Missouri. He said he knew his father's side of the family was from St. Louis, but he didn't know them. Meanwhile, I majored in accounting, and Kane majored in cyber security with a minor in game design. I got a job right out of undergrad with US Bank while he continued with his master's in cyber security. We were friends throughout our college days and remained friends after we graduated. It wasn't until a couple of months before he finished his graduate degree that we declared ourselves a couple.

    Everything had been going well in our relationship the past six years. Plus the sex was still beyond amazing. It wasn't until he was fired from his job at Dexter Regis Technologies that things began to go downhill for us a little. Him and two other employees were fired for a major security breach, and the company was now facing a pending lawsuit from some of its clients. I felt sorry for Kane and the other two employees because I knew it was an honest accident, but it was a major fuckup on their parts. He's been having a hard time getting a job because of this, but I figured something would come through eventually.

I missed what we had. The date nights and trips out of town have come to halt because we couldn't really afford to do much anymore. Hell, we couldn't really afford to order from Door Dash tonight, but it is what it is. I sighed as I stepped out the shower and grabbed a towel to wrap around myself. I wiped the fog off the mirror and observed my facial features. I could definitely say that I was a catch with a pretty, round face, big eyes, and full lips. I was roughly the same caramel complexion as Kane, and my eyes were more of a light brown. I was on the plus side, proudly wearing a size eighteen, and Kane said he found it sexy that I was thick and plenty for him. I chuckled as I thought about how he'd always say that to me. I was very confident in myself, and I figured that all my curves were a plus anyway.

I went into our bedroom and sat on the bed to lotion myself down. Kane came into the room and threw on what he called rags, I'd assume to cut the grass. I gave him my sexy look, and he bit his bottom lip. I was feeling a little frisky, and I could tell he was on board. Unfortunately, my phone rang, and it threw us off. I would have ignored it, but I programmed a special ringtone for my mother, and I knew that if I didn't answer, she would keep calling me back.

My mother suffered from a traumatic brain injury when she had a car accident a few years ago. I was sixteen years old, and my brother Alan was nineteen years old when the injury happened. She was in the hospital for a month and was sent to a rehab facility for a few months after that. To make matters worse, my father was in Iraq when this happened. Ironically, he was killed by a roadside bomb within a couple of days of mother's accident. I'm not sure who opened their mouth, but Children's Division got involved because I was still a minor and practically raising myself. I figured that was a bunch of bullshit, but I guess the law was going to prevail regardless.

Alan had moved out our home about a year before to live with his girlfriend, an older woman. However, he agreed to move back in to our parents' house so they wouldn't try to remove me from the home. It seemed it would have been easier for me to just move in with him, but apparently, his girlfriend wasn't having that. After six months, my mother was released from the rehab facility to come home and into Alan's care. He moved out and right back in with his girlfriend within barely a month of her being home, and I was left alone to care for my mother.

I felt like Alan was wrong as hell for that, but I will say that he did well handling the finances, since he became our mother's payee for her social-security benefits as well as the payee for my father's death benefits. He spent the money from my father's life-insurance policy wisely as well by paying off the house. He didn't keep a dime of the money, made sure all the leftover funds went to taking care of the bills, and the rest came to me. Overall, my life was stressful with the death of my father and illness of my mother, but I survived.

"Hello?" I answered, a little annoyed. She was my mother, and I loved her dearly, but I already knew she didn't want much of anything.

"Almi?" she asked, like she always did, as if it

would be someone else answering my phone. I used to hate my name, but over the years, a lot of people have told me that it was beautiful. It was pronounced *all me*, and my father said he named me that because he could instantly see I was a spitting image of him from the day I was born. He was right, because I looked just like a female version of him.

"Yeah, it's me, Ma," I replied.

"Hi, baby. I was just calling to tell you I was watching the news, and as usual, there's some crazy things happening in this God-forsaken city of ours," she said.

"I know, Mama. Just the same old mess," I told her, getting a little impatient. I was trying to get back to getting freaky with Kane before I lost the entire mood I was in.

"I wish this world wasn't so crazy. It's a shame how these folks act," she stated.

"Hey, Mama, can I call you back later?" I asked her.

"You know, baby, I wish things would go back to the way they used to be. I wish you would come back home, and Alan too. Both of y'all and like… you know…

come live with me again. That would be nice, don't you think?" she continued talking, ignoring my request to call her back.

"Yeah, that would be nice, but I'm grown now, Mama. I have to live on my own."

"It would be great. You, Alan, me, and your father. It's a shame he never came back home. What does he like so much about Iraq that he never came back home to his family?" she asked.

Every time she brought up my father it brought tears to my eyes. I missed him so much. I knew she missed him too. We told her several times that he had passed away, but either her brain just couldn't process what I told her, or she refused to believe it. With a traumatic brain injury, it was so hard to tell what she understood and what she didn't.

"Mama, please let me just call you back." I sighed, already over wanting to have sex with Kane. I was no longer in the mood now since I was feeling sad.

"Don't forget. You always forget," she said.

"I won't, Mama. I'll call you," I told her, hanging

up.

"I wish you wouldn't do your mother like that," Kane said, shaking his head at me as soon as I put the phone down.

"You wouldn't understand. You don't know how stressful it is dealing with her being ill," I said with tears falling from my eyes.

"I know it's not easy, but she's the only mother you have. She doesn't mean any harm." He tried to reason with me.

"Just leave it alone. OK?" I said to him.

He shrugged and left our bedroom. I flopped down on the bed and cried. I was thirty and figured I had done pretty well for myself so far. I had my dream job, drove a nice car, and shared a beautiful home with Kane. However, it seemed like things were falling apart in my life. I worked so hard to get where I am today, but I was starting to lose my mind.

While we still had mind-blowing sex whenever we did, my love life was beginning to suffer with Kane because our moments together were becoming few and far in between. My mama seemed to need me more and more, causing my anxiety to be at an all-time high. Not to mention the demands of my job was pulling me in a million directions. I was so stressed out that I had suffered a miscarriage two months ago, but now wouldn't have been the time to try raising a child anyway. I knew there were people in this world who were far worse off than me, but I just wanted one twenty-four-hour day not to have a worry in the world. I was so tired of being everyone else's strength. I wished someone could hold me up for a change while I was down. I was slowly but surely losing myself, and sometimes I didn't know who I was anymore.

Chapter 2 Kane

I swear that sometimes Almi made me feel like I was less than a man for not working. I wanted to work, I promise I did, but things just weren't going in my favor right now. No one was willing to hire me once they learned I was responsible for a major security breach at Dexter Regis Technologies. That was my first job right out of graduate school, and even though I considered leaving them off my resume, that wouldn't get me too far either. Potential jobs always wanted to know where you previously worked and wanted you to account for any time of unemployment. It was a no-win situation for me, unless I decided to switch gears and try working in another field. With no education or experience in anything else, I was left to work some dead-end job. It looked like that's what my future was going to consist of because I couldn't stay out of work too much longer.

Almi thought I sat around on my video game all day, but I didn't. I put in applications and sent resumes out online, only to keep getting declined for interviews. The human resource representatives from the two interviews I went on in the past couple of weeks told me they would get back with me, but I haven't heard anything. I was sure they tossed my application to the side once they got reference information back from Dexter Regis. I didn't bother to tell Almi these things because I didn't want her sympathy. Things were hard enough dealing with rejection without my woman's looks of pity. Instead of her asking, she just assumed I was up to nothing. I loved her with my all, but I was seeing another side of her now that I didn't have a job. I felt like I was beneath her, and that was the worse feeling in the world.

With her income and what we had in savings, we had enough to survive for another four months. She was ready to buy a house a few months ago, but I'm glad we didn't because look what happened. I wanted to suggest we downsize from our bungalow-style house to an apartment that we could actually afford. I was always taught by my mother to live off one income because you never knew what could happen. I wish I could tell Almi that, but all she would ever say is how hard she worked to get where she is today, and she refused to go backward. I wouldn't say it was going backward, but I felt it would be a good step to take toward living smarter.

I grew tired of playing the game and decided to head into the kitchen to take something out to cook. She made me feel bad last week when she said the least bit I could do was have dinner prepared. She did have a point. I took out the bag of grilled chicken pieces and began chopping up onion and peppers so I could prepare us some chicken fajitas for dinner. I found a box of brown rice and figured we might as well have that on the side. I thanked my lucky stars when I opened the cabinet and saw a bottle of wine as well. I didn't really feel up to running out to the store to purchase any, and I didn't want to ask her to stop on the way home. I wanted to surprise her and allow her to walk in to me pampering her for a change.

I finished up dinner right before five p.m. and knew she should be walking through the door soon. I decided to run her a steaming-hot bath so she could relax and soak away the stress from her workday. She would always say she wasn't a fan of baths and preferred to take showers, but I didn't think anything was wrong with a nice bubble bath every once in a while. I lit her a couple of the Champagne Toast candles she got from Bath & Body Works and put on some jazz music for her. She was a huge fan of jazz while studying in college and said her dad would always play jazz or blues music while they cleaned up Saturday mornings, so it kind of grew on her.

I sat on the sofa and tried to find something to watch on the Fire Stick while I waited for Almi to come in. When I heard her car finally pull into the driveway right after 5:30 p.m., I smiled. I couldn't wait to see the smile on her face when she walked through the door and saw that I had dinner ready for her. I stood up to meet her at the door so I could greet her with a hug and kiss.

"Hey bae," I said, as I opened the door.

"Hey, you." She smiled, kissing me passionately. She inhaled, and I could tell she was curious about the food she smelled.

"Yes, I made us chicken fajitas and rice for dinner. Go ahead and relax in the bubble bath I ran for you while I fix our plates," I told her, kissing her again.

"Aw, Kane. Thank you, baby," she said. "I'm

doing everything I can not to mess up the mood, but you do know I don't take baths right?"

"Well, you are today," I said her, taking her work bag and purse out of her hand and placing them on the kitchen counter.

"I guess you're right then." She chuckled.

I watched and licked my lips as she switched away. I couldn't wait to feel her warm insides tonight. I loved how her pussy hugged my dick perfectly and how intense her moans always sounded when I pounded in and out of her sweet spot. My dick grew hard and jumped as I thought about it. We had to get through dinner first, and then it was on after that.

As I scooped rice on our plates, my cell phone vibrated with a text message. It was my boy Perry calling to invite me out for the evening. He said he wanted us to catch up and shoot some pool at Classics tonight. I wanted to take him up on that offer, but I had some making up to do with Almi. I shot him a text back declining his offer. The message barely said sent before he was calling my phone.

"What's good, man?" I answered.

"I decided to bypass the text messaging and just hit you up. I already knew you would come with some bullshit excuse," he said.

"It's not bullshit. I've been tripping a little bit lately and slacking around the crib, man. I gotta show Almi that I appreciate her holding things down while I'm trying to get my life back on track. We can get together next time," I told him.

"That's the whole point. There won't be a next time. I just accepted a job in Chicago today, and I'm leaving next week. I'm not doing some big going away party but just wanted to catch up with a couple of the people I'm close to," Perry said.

"Damn, man! You about to straight leave me here in the Lou!" I exclaimed.

"I gotta do what I gotta do. This is a good opportunity, and I can't pass it up," he said.

"I feel you," I replied. I met Perry when we attended Maryville University. We were roommates in Duschesne Hall and became pretty good friends. We've damn near been joined at the hip since. I hated the idea of my boy leaving, but I was also happy for him. "How soon are you leaving?" I asked him.

"I already said next week. Listen, man!" He chuckled. "I'm leaving Monday morning."

"Damn, man! It's Thursday. Why so soon?"

"Life waits on no one. The company I'll be working for found me an apartment, and they're paying for my first six months of rent. I'm leaving Monday so I can move and settled in because I start work the following week. They need me up there anyway to attend orientation next Wednesday," he said.

"I guess I ain't got no choice but to catch up with you tonight then. What time are you talking about?" I asked, hoping I'd still have time to romance my woman.

"In about an hour," he said.

"Alright." I sighed, knowing that was completely throwing off my plans with Almi. I was sure she'd understand, or at least I hoped she would. "I'll see you in a minute."

We hung up the phone, and I regretted having to

tell her that I had to head out after dinner. I was sure she'd only think I did all of this as my way of springing this on her. There was no way she'd believe this came up out of nowhere. Almi normally didn't care about me hanging out, but with me not working and her complaining that we haven't spent much time together lately, I knew she'd bitch a fit about this. I just had to play this situation smooth, or it could blow up to world war three.

I sat down at the table after pouring each of us a glass of wine. I played over and over in my head how I was going to tell her and figured the best thing to do was to just come right out and let her know I was heading out tonight with Perry because he was going away. I damn near changed my mind when Almi's sexy ass sashayed into the kitchen wearing a turquoise, silk teddy. My manhood jumped, and I was seconds away from just wishing Perry well and telling him I'd catch him the next time he was in town, but I knew I couldn't do that. Instead, I smiled and licked my lips. I couldn't let this moment go to waste, so I figured it wouldn't hurt if I ran a few minutes late getting to the sports bar. There were plenty of pool tables, so we'd be straight.

I got up and stuck my tongue down her throat while cupping her round ass in my both of my hands. I gave it squeeze and enjoyed the moan that escaped her lips. I traced my tongue to her neck and gently sank my teeth into her flesh, making her moan a little louder.

"H-H-Hold on, bae," she whispered. "We have plenty of time for dessert after we finish dinner."

I sighed and pulled away because I knew I wasn't about to get none now. I hated being in this position where I had to choose between showing up for my boy or being here for my woman. I done seen enough of this shit in movies to know this was not going to go over well at all. I shook my head and took a seat.

"What's wrong, baby?" Almi asked, noticing the change in my mood.

"Nothing, bae," I replied quietly.

She took a seat and smiled as she took in the feast before her. "I appreciate you fixing dinner tonight," she said as she took a sip of her wine.

"Anything for you, baby," I replied, working on

easing her in for the kill.

"I have something extra special for you tonight to show you my appreciation." She winked.

"Um… about that…" I almost hesitated to say. She raised her eyebrows in anticipation of me finishing my thought. "Perry just contacted me and told me he was taking a job out of town and leaving as soon as a couple of days from now. He wanted to meet with me and a couple of the fellas at Classics tonight as a little going-away gathering type of thing," I told her.

She shrugged as she took a bite of her food. "Have fun, I guess," she said nonchalantly. That was not the reaction I was expecting at all. Part of me was relieved we didn't have to argue, but a slight part of me was worried too. That was not a typical reaction from her, so now I was wondering what was up her sleeve.

"That's it?" I asked, immediately regretting that I asked. *What type of shit was that, Kane? You wanna be off the hook or not?*

"Was there supposed to be more?" she inquired a bit sarcastically.

"Nah, I'm just surprised you're so easy going about it."

"Oh, so am I normally difficult?"

"Nah, bae, I was just... never mind. Thank you for understanding. I promise I won't be out late at all," I told her.

"Take your time. Have fun," she said, getting up from the table and heading into our room.

I could tell that she was pissed off. She was just playing it cool for now. I already knew this would mean the silent treatment later, and I definitely wasn't getting no ass tonight. I hated when shit had to play out like this. Part of me felt like she was acting childish because this was something we could talk about and come to an understanding like mature adults. However, I also understood her feelings were hurt. She was expecting a romantic night, and she even got sexy for me to tell her I was pushing it off for a couple of hours. I was sure that by tomorrow, everything would be fine between us, and I was going to make sure to give her my all. Tomorrow was the weekend, and I was making it a full weekend just about her.

After I got dressed to leave, I walked over to Almi lying on the bed to give her a kiss. Her eyes were closed, and she looked so angelic and peaceful. I just kissed her forehead softly so I wouldn't disturb her rest. I loved this woman with every fiber of my being, and I wanted things to get better for us. I made a promise to see to it that I gave her the world, and she would know how much I loved and appreciated her. I just needed her to be patient with me for a little while longer while I looked for a job. Things were going to get better.

I continued to feel guilty as I drove to Classics, but that quickly dissipated when I saw Perry and the rest of the crew outside waiting for me. When I got out the car, we started this little chant we used to do back in our college days and dapped each other up when we were finished. None of us bothered to join a fraternity because we had formed our own brotherhood. I wasn't against fraternities or anything. It just wasn't my cup of tea. Meanwhile, I was content with the folks I allowed in my circle, and no new friends were needed.

We went inside and ordered a couple pitchers of beer, chicken wings, and pizza. We got a pool game going immediately, and the fun had begun. Perry and I played against our homeboys Raynell and Buffalo. We lost, but I can't say that I was mad because I was just happy to be out with my boys. It had been a while since I had a chance to catch up with them because I was going through a bout of depression since losing my job. It was about time I started getting back to my old self and start enjoying life again. I was still determined to find a job and get things back on the good foot with Almi, but I also needed to take care of my mental health and not lose myself completely.

After we finished our game, I went to the bar to order a shot of Hennessy. While I waited for the bartender to fix my drink, Buffalo came over to tell me goodnight because he had to get home to his wife. Raynell was on the opposite side of the bar caking with some woman, and I noticed Perry with his phone to his ear heading toward the door. I was certain he wasn't leaving without saying goodbye but was probably taking the call outside since there was no way he could hear over the noise in here. When the bartender handed me my drink, I knocked it back immediately. I was about to order another one when a woman took a seat next to me and winked.

"Slow down a little," she teased.

"I'm a pro. I got this," I told her, observing her beautiful features. She had a cute, little, button nose, full lips, and a dark-skinned complexion. Her hair flowed evenly down her back, and she had the prettiest white teeth. I had to shake my head to refocus and stop drooling over this woman.

"I hear you. I was just looking out for you." She giggled.

"I appreciate that, but I'm good," I told her.

She shrugged and ordered a sex on the beach. That used to be one of Almi's favorite drinks until she said no one ordered those anymore. Apparently, she was wrong because this goddess before me certainly ordered one and had proven Almi completely wrong.

"You here alone?" she asked. I could swear she was flirting, and maybe she was, or maybe it was that shot of Hennessy that had me tripping.

"I'm here with my boys," I told her.

"Where are they?" she asked, looking around as if she didn't believe me.

"They're around."

"Oh OK, Mr. Smarty Pants." She smiled.

"Look, I'm in a serious relationship, and I'm only trying to stop anything before it can begin." I decided to be straightforward with her.

"I'm very glad that you're confident in yourself, but absolutely nothing was going to begin. I was just holding a friendly conversation," she replied.

"My apologies," I said quietly. My ego was bruised, but I guess rightfully so for making that assumption.

"OK, OK. You got me. I actually was flirting. I think you're cute, but I can certainly respect that you're a taken man. I'm no home-wrecker, and I know my place." She threw her hands up defensively.

"There's nothing wrong with friendly conversation. I was just putting it out there so there wouldn't be any misunderstandings later."

"I know when to fall back. I get it."

"How are you today though?" I asked, trying to change the subject. I couldn't lie, shorty was bad as hell, and I was drawn to her. I wasn't going to cross that line of disrespect though. I was going to enjoy conversing with her for now, and when we walked out of these doors tonight, that was it.

About twenty minutes into our conversation, Perry and Raynell let me know they were leaving, so I figured I might as well call it a night as well.

"It was nice meeting you," I told her as I got up to leave.

"It was nice meeting you too…" She let her voice trail off as I realized we never exchanged names.

"Kane," I told her.

"As in Cain and Abel?" she asked.

"No, as in K-A-N-E," I replied.

"That's different, but I like it. I'm Zavia," she informed me.

"It was a pleasure speaking with you. Have a good night," I said.

"You too, Kane. Maybe I'll see you around," she suggested.

"Nah, I don't get out much."

"Well, you should change that. I really enjoyed chatting with you. Let me know the next time you plan to come here, and I'll look for you. Don't worry, I'll keep it friendly. I really meant it when I said about respecting your relationship."

She gave me her number, and I knew I shouldn't have taken it, but I did. I told myself that I absolutely was not going to cheat. I sent her a text message telling her to lock my number in and that we'd chat soon. On the drive home, I thought about Zavia, but I released her from my thoughts as I pulled into my driveway. I was hoping Almi felt generous and would let me slide in her. I needed to feel her warmth around my dick.

As I let myself in, a message request notification came to my Facebook Messenger. I looked at it and saw that it was someone asking me to contact him. I raised my eyebrows when I recognized the name. Years ago, I had asked my mother my father's name. She told me one time and said to never ask his name again. I guess I would give Mr. Wesley Clayton a call in the morning to see what he could possibly want after all of these years.

Chapter 3 Almi

I collapsed on my bed, pulled my knees to my chest, and held myself in a fetal position. I closed my eyes, started counting backward from one hundred, and willed my heart to stop beating so profusely. I opened my eyes for a moment, only to get dizzy by the room spinning faster and faster. I did my best to take deep breaths and kept telling myself that I was alright. After a couple of minutes, I noticed my heart rate slowing, and my breathing began returning to normal. I slowly got out of the bed and stumbled to the dresser to get my Hydroxyzine pills. I struggled with the bottle for a minute, but finally got it opened and took one. I sat back down on the bed and swallowed a huge gulp from the bottle of water I had sitting on the nightstand. I wasn't sure what triggered that panic attack, but all I could do was lie down for a moment and wait for this medicine to kick in.

I must have dozed off without realizing it, because I was awakened by Kane kissing my forehead. I damn near jumped out of my skin but smiled when I saw it was him. I was still a little upset with him from last night, but it was hard to stay mad at him forever. Besides, he had already made it up to me by doing the laundry and running a couple of errands for me. When I came in from work, he had dinner prepared again. He told me to pick out a movie for us to watch while he ran out to get us some snacks. It was my intention to do that, but after having that panic attack, I had to lie down for a minute and never got around to it. I figured it would be nice to pick the movie out together anyway.

He pulled me off the bed and into his arms. It felt good to be loved by this man, and I could only hope that things would get better from here. I was going to remain positive and be confident that we were only going through a temporary storm at this time. Things could only go up from here, because I felt we had already hit rock bottom as a couple. Our relationship wasn't bad. It was just being tested lately with what's been going on. There was no point in giving up and throwing away what we had.

Once we were seated on our couch, I snuggled up closer to him and kissed his cheek. We were holding hands, and he gave mine a squeeze. I felt like a teenager in love and wanted to be in this moment with him forever. We scrolled through the Fire Stick to find something to watch, but his cell phone rang and grabbed his attention. I noticed how he scrunched his face up when he saw who was calling, but I was even more perturbed when he excused himself. *What part of the game was this? Since when did we start leaving the room to take phone calls?*

I sat there and continued scrolling through the movie selections, trying not to be bothered by his actions. My heart started racing, and my ears perked up when I heard him laughing. *Who the hell had my man's attention and was making him laugh like some shit was really that damn funny?* I tried ear hustling so I could hear his side of the conversation but was unsuccessful because his voice dipped low. I sat there for a couple more minutes before I said fuck it and walked into the room where he was. I put my hands on my hips, and I'm sure by the look on my face he could see that I very displeased by what was taking place. Once he got the hint, he quickly ended the call and apologized.

"What's wrong with you?" he asked like he really

didn't know.

"Since when did we start walking away from each other to talk on the phone? Was there something you didn't want me to hear?" I inquired.

"It's nothing like that, baby. Chill. Let's go watch our movie," he suggested, getting off the bed to walk out of the bedroom and back into the living room.

"Who was that anyway?" I wanted to know.

"It was nobody." He shrugged.

"So nobody has you laughing like what the fuck she said was really that damn funny, huh?" I snapped.

"What makes you think it was a female? Why are you tripping?"

"Why are you being so secretive?"

"Just leave it alone, Almi. It wasn't a female. Damn!" he yelled out.

If he wasn't guilty, why else would he be getting so upset? He plopped down on the sofa and told Alexa to go to YouTube on the Fire Stick. He commanded she play Gerald Levert "Made to Love Ya", and I smiled because that was our song. I shook my head but didn't resist when he smiled as well and took my hand to dance with him. He had a way of making me instantly forgive him because he knew just how to woo me in. Again, enjoying the present moment with him, I relaxed and began to think positive again. I was sure I was getting upset over nothing, especially since Kane had never given me a reason not to trust him. Our dance turned into nothing more than us making out very passionately before our clothes began to come off.

By then, 112 started singing about wanting to make sweet love, and that's exactly what we did as we made our way to the bedroom. Music continued to play over the surround-sound speakers as Kane and I found a rhythm of our own. He began stroking in and out of me while I was on all fours. The palm of his hand came across my ass, causing it to jiggle. I hissed from the pain of pleasure he caused when his hand hit my flesh, and I arched my back even more. I felt him slide his dick out, and I begged him to re-enter me. He slowly began sliding back in but continued to tease me by only letting his dick head sit at the tip of my love hole. I looked over my shoulder at him as he sucked his thumb before sticking it into that forbidden place. He pursed his lips, letting his hot saliva ooze and fall in a stream as it hit his dick. He pushed his thumb further into my ass, causing me to moan louder.

He finally pushed his dick the rest of the way into me and began to speed up. He kept my ass cheeks spread apart with one hand with his thumb still in me. He worked me over and began to mercilessly beat my pussy up. I continued to moan, and my lip quivered as he hit my G-spot. My pussy began squirting juices, and I screamed out for him not to stop. He continued to deliver powerful thrusts with his big, pretty, brown dick. I felt my eyes roll into the back of my head as my body began to jerk and shiver from the orgasm he drew out of me. I collapsed on the bed, and he collapsed on top me, continuing to stroke me slowly. He began sucking the back of my neck and whispered in my ear that he was about to cum. Once he released, I was ready to doze off. I was sexually satisfied from the amazing lovemaking Kane had just given me. I promise this man could do no wrong in my eyes. I just hoped he didn't make a fool of me in the long run, and I'd feel this way about him forever.

Chapter 4 Kane

I knew I shouldn't, but it was hard to decline the offer to meet with Zavia at Starbucks. It was only two people building a friendship, so our meeting should be harmless. However, I knew if Almi found out about this, she would pissed off, and rightfully so. I had to admit to myself that I wouldn't be too thrilled to hear about Almi meeting up with another man for a cup of coffee either. I needed a quick breakthrough.

It seemed things were starting to flow better for us, especially after that good dick I put down on her the other night, but the next morning, she was back to being the grumpy person she's been lately. As she had become accustomed to doing, she made me feel low and constantly reminded me that I wasn't working. I was doing my best to change that, but instead of her encouraging me, she seemed to belittle me.

I sat near the back of the cafe with the hopes of not running into anyone, because you just didn't know. To be on the safe side, I had already taken the extra precaution of coming all the way out to a Starbucks location in St.

Charles, Missouri. Almi worked at an accounting firm in Creve Coeur, which wasn't too far, but it would still be unusual to run into her or one of her co-workers way out here. Zavia didn't seem to question why I wanted to come so far out, but she just went with the flow of things. It's not like she didn't know I had a woman, which is probably why she didn't question it.

"Well, look at what the wind finally blew in," I said as she rushed to the table where we were sitting. She called on her way here and told me to order a Grande salted-caramel frappe, and I had it waiting for her. It was a little nippy outside today, and I had no idea why she wanted a cold drink, but to each his own. I settled on something warmer to give a little heat to my chilled bones. I was enjoying a caramel-mocha latte right now with extra whipped cream.

"I couldn't believe the traffic that was on Interstate 70 coming over the bridge out here. I was like, 'damn, do these people even work that they're out driving the damn highway in the middle of the day?'" She laughed.

I let out a slight chuckle, but didn't find her joke

too amusing. Just because they were out driving didn't mean they didn't work. Those folks could have been on lunch break, off work, self-employed, or had a later shift to work. Her assumption was a horrible one, but I didn't want to let it damper the mood.

"So tell me a little more about yourself," I said to her, changing the subject.

"I work as an adjunct instructor at Columbia College where I teach a communications course," she said.

"That sounds like an interesting career," I replied. "What made you become a college professor?"

"Well, see, I'm not a professor, but an instructor. A professor requires a doctoral degree, which I'm currently working on," she stated.

"I got you. You still didn't answer my question about what made you want to teach," I told her.

"Teaching was actually far from my mind. I used to write for a local newspaper when I lived in Cape Girardeau. After I finished my bachelor's degree in journalism, that was my first job out of college. I'm originally from St. Louis and wanted to come back home after a couple of years of working down there. The small-town living wasn't really for me. Of course I had to have a job to come home to, and this particular job was the one I saw an opening for as close to my field as I could get, so applied."

"You mentioned you were working on your doctoral degree. What is your master's degree in?"

"I got my bachelor's degree in communication arts from Webster University. A guy I was dating at the time moved to Cape Girardeau, so I moved down there with him and decided to attend graduate school at Southeast Missouri State. My master's is in English and professional writing. We broke up a couple of months before I graduated, and I had to branch out on my own. I stayed there for a couple of years, but as I mentioned, living there permanently was not in my plans."

"I grew up in Kansas City, and I got bored with being there too, which is what brought me to St. Louis. My mother was from here, and my father's side of the family was from here too, so I figured this wouldn't be a bad place to start my adult life. I don't care for the high crime rate,

51

but crime is everywhere when you really think about it."

"Yeah and no," she said, scrunching up her face. "I must admit that Cape Girardeau was definitely more peaceful. I don't even recall hearing about a murder but maybe a couple of times the entire time I was there. It's become the norm here, and I'm more shocked *not* to hear about one."

"I guess you have a point." I shrugged, taking a sip of my drink.

"What about you?" she inquired.

"What about me?" I wondered. She had thrown me completely off with that question.

"Where do you work?" she asked.

"I'm currently unemployed, but I'm looking," I told her.

"Oh," she said, raising her eyebrows.

"It's not what you think. I'm not some bum ass dude. I have my graduate degree from Maryville University in cyber security. I was previously employed by Dexter Regis Technologies until they let me go."

"Oh, you were one of the three responsible for that

52

security breach," she said knowingly.

Now was my turn to raise my eyebrow. "Um… yeah," I said.

"It was all over the news when it happened," she replied, confirming my suspicion when she saw I wondered how she could possibly know about what happened at Dexter Regis.

"Unfortunately." I sighed.

"So you still haven't found another job?"

I could have sworn I just said that. "Nah, not yet. I've been looking."

"Well, how would you like to become an instructor at Columbia College? There are a couple of openings for computer-science instructors. Your degree would make you a great candidate."

"I seriously doubt Columbia College would consider me."

"I have a little pull," she suggested, taking a sip of her drink.

"Don't get me all excited for nothing," I said with doubt.

"I wouldn't even do you like that. You seem like a nice person. Just email me your resume, get you a couple of references together, and give me a couple of days to get back with you."

"You don't even know me for real. Why are you so willing to help me?"

"Like I said, you seem like a really nice guy. Just see it as a friend helping out a friend."

"I appreciate it," I told her, looking at my phone and seeing that she had already text me her email address. "I'll get that to you by the end of the day."

We finished up our drinks and continued to talk for a few more minutes. She said she had to get back to work but would be in touch with me soon.

I continued sitting there for a moment as I watched her get up from the table and walk away. I admired her beauty, and I would be lying if I said I didn't lust after her as I observed her shapely body. I guess there was no harm in meeting with Zavia after all. We conducted ourselves like mature adults, and now it looked like I may be getting a job. It seemed our friendship would do more good than harm. As I thought more about what my future may possibly hold if I got this job, my phone rang. It was my father calling. I called him the other day, and it looked like he was finally returning my call.

"Hello?" I answered.

"Hi, is this Kane?" the man on the other line asked.

"Yes, this is he. How may I help you?" I asked him, wondering what it was my father could possibly want after all these years.

"This is Wesley Clayton, your father," he replied, as if I didn't already know who he was.

"Like I said, how may I help you?"

"I'm sure this is a shock to hear from me after all these years. There is no point in me giving some long, drawn-out speech about why I wasn't there for you. All I know is we're in the present, and I would like to get a chance to meet you son, and see if we can go from there."

I hesitated before I spoke. He had a lot of fucking audacity to pop up out of nowhere and think we could possibly start a father-son relationship after all these years. Yet deep down this was something I always yearned for.

He missed so much of my life, and there were times I needed a father, but he was not there for me. He was right though. This was the present, and we couldn't live in the past. I figured since we still had breath in our bodies, we might as well get the chance to know each other now.

"I guess that will be alright," I finally answered after a few seconds.

"Good. Can we arrange a day and time to meet?"

"When did you have in mind?" I asked, still surprised I was allowing myself to go along with this.

"How about some time next week. I'll be free then to sit down for a few days and catch up with you."

Considering I was very unemployed at the moment, I obviously had a lot of time on my hands for whenever he had time to meet. "That will work," I agreed.

"I'll be in touch. I look forward to meeting you."

"Likewise," I said before hanging up.

Little did he or my mother know, I had done some research on my father over the years. Mr. Wesley Clayton was one of the most wealthiest men in St. Louis, Missouri. He operated a rental management company where he owned over thirty properties himself, in addition to managing properties for other landlords. My father had bread, and not that I really *needed* him for anything, but it probably wouldn't hurt to figure out how beneficial a father-son relationship may prove to be after all. This could be quite a lucrative investment on my part.

Chapter 5 Almi

I sat in my office tapping away at the keys and looking at the computer screen as I entered information into our system for one of our new clients. I worked as a senior accountant for Fabian Brown Accounting Services, one of the most successful, and black-owned accounting firms in not only our city, but the country. This was my second job I got about a year after working for US Bank, when I finished my undergraduate degree. I was always excited about getting new clients, especially right before the holidays, because those appreciation gifts and packages were always nice.

The year before last, I got a new client in late October who owned a travel agency. They were so satisfied with the work that I had done in only two months, that they gave me a paid vacation for two to Maui, Hawaii. It was a weeklong vacation, so that's where Kane and I spent our 2016 Christmas and 2017 New Year. Last year, another client offered for me to purchase a new car from his luxury dealership for 75% off. Yes, I got a brand new 2017 Infiniti Q70 for only $12,500. The new client I was working on now, Queen Fletcher Publishing, was one of the largest book and magazine publishing companies in the country, found right here in St. Louis, Missouri. I was excited about having her file because she was known to organize some of the best events. One of her books series, *Hope for A Misfit*, had recently been turned into a movie. There was also talk about turning her book *R.E.A.L. (Remember Everybody Ain't Loyal)* into a movie as well, so I could only imagine the perks she'd offer me for handling her finances.

A knock came at my door, interrupting my flow. My door was already halfway open, and I could see another senior accountant standing there with someone standing to the side. I barely looked up from my screen, but I at least spoke to acknowledge them and let them know I saw them there.

"Yes," I replied, still entering figures into the system.

"Almi, this is Marshall. Marshall is the young man Mr. Brown said would be starting with us today. He was supposed to be shadowing me this week, but one of my clients called an emergency meeting in Phoenix first thing tomorrow that they need me to attend. I'm about to head home in a few so I can pack and get a flight out in a couple of hours. Mr. Brown wanted me to check with you to see if you wouldn't mind him shadowing you instead," my co-worker Misty asked me.

I cut her a look so she'd know I was not pleased about her putting me on the spot. She could have come asked me this alone, especially if I decided to tell him no. I rolled my eyes, still not looking Marshall's way. "I guess," I mumbled.

"I really appreciate it, Ms. Almi," a deep voice spoke up.

That *miss* crap in my name made me feel old, so I had to set him straight right now. "Almi is fi—" I started to say, but stopped when I finally looked at him. The man who stood before me was fine as hell. He was dark-skinned, stood about six feet tall, with a strong jaw bones, sexy lips, and gray eyes. He wore his hair cut low with waves like Kane did. *Kane*... I almost forgot about my boyfriend after indulging in this eye candy before me.

60

Don't get me wrong, I came across fine men all the time, but Marshall was too damn fine for no reason. His sexiness should be a crime. He looked so delicious that they ought to lock him up and throw away the key to preserve that dark chocolate forever.

"Almi without the *miss* is fine." I finished what I started to say once I regained control of myself.

"Again, thank you, Almi." Marshall smiled, arousing something down on the inside of me.

"No problem. Let me finish up what I'm working on, and we can get started on something you can observe from the first steps. Does that sound alright to you?" I asked him.

"Do your thing. I'm on your time," he replied.

For some reason, I became extra nervous as I felt Marshall's eyes watching me intently. I don't know how many times I had to backspace to correct a few errors. This definitely was not good for business. I had to carefully review everything I put into the system to make sure I didn't mess up on this new account. Once I was satisfied that everything was in order, I closed out that screen on my computer and gave Marshall my undivided attention.

"So where would you like to begin? Did you already get your tour of the office?" I asked him.

"I had a brief tour on the day I interviewed, but I wouldn't mind another quick one as a refresher. The interview was almost a month ago," he said.

"An entire month ago? It took that long for you to get started?"

"Apparently so. I understand though. Mr. Brown is a busy man, and this is one of the most prestigious accounting firms around. I'm just glad to finally have my foot in the door. I've had other mediocre accounting firms turn me down, so to be pulled in here is an honor."

I smiled and nodded my head in agreement as I stepped from behind my desk and smoothed out my skirt. I gestured for him to follow me. As he walked behind me, I could feel his eyes burning a hole through me. I don't know why, but I threw a little extra switch in my step to give him something more to appreciate. *You're tripping, girl. Do you remember your boyfriend Kane?*

"So is accounting your only background?" I asked

him, once we arrived in the break room. I went to pour myself a cup of coffee, and he followed suit.

"Yes. I started as an accountant for a grocery store right out of college a few years ago. I felt, with my experience and skills, it was time to advance to something further. I've been trying to leave my last job for about six months, so as I mentioned, I am definitely happy to have this opportunity."

"As you should be. This is a great firm to work for."

"Believe me, I know," he replied, following me out of the break room.

He continued to walk behind me like a lost puppy, which actually began to irk me a little. I felt man should always lead or at least walk beside you, not behind you. It made him look weak in my opinion. After showing him our miniature library and fitness center, I made sure to walk a little more slowly, so I could walk alongside him.

"How long have you been working here?" he asked me.

"About eight years now. This was my second after finishing my undergrad," I told him.

63

"Really? That's impressive you got right in," he gushed.

"Not quite. Mr. Brown was actually just starting out and had only had his company for about two years. He's grown quite well over the past few years though, has won several awards, and an extremely great client base."

"So you're part of the roots, huh?"

"That seems fair to say." I shrugged, not wanting to come off as arrogant, even though he was the one who said it.

Once we finished our tour, we ended right back up at my office. I informed him that I had a couple of calls to make to my clients, and he was more than welcome to observe how I communicated with them. The right verbiage was particularly important when maintaining rapport and trust. I was sure with his experience he knew all about communication, but then again, who knows? He worked directly for the grocery store chain who hired him. At Fabian Brown, he'd deal with a variety of outside clients and business will be handled in multiple ways.

There Marshall was again, watching me with those

sexy eyes as I spoke with Elizabeth Strong Photography LLC. I don't know why, but he made me a little nervous, and I found myself stumbling over my words. I was making a complete ass of myself when I was supposed to be setting an example. Thankfully, I had been dealing with this client for a couple of years, and she'd probably just chalk it up to me having a bad day. At least I hoped so.

I don't know what it was about Marshall that had me tripping all over myself. Hell, Kane couldn't even do that. It didn't help that Marshall was watching me so intently and kept licking his lips. I promise this man was undressing me with his eyes, and it made me feel self-conscious all of a sudden. I hurriedly tried to finish the call so I could hang up. When I did, I took a huge gulp from my water bottle sitting on my desk. I was a little embarrassed from the water that dripped off my lip because Marshall chuckled a little.

"If you don't mind my asking, why are you staring me like that?" I asked him.

"I don't want to seem out of place, so forgive me ahead of time. It's just that, Almi, I think you are a very beautiful woman. You're very educated as well, and I can only imagine how lucky the man in your life must be." He flirted.

"I'm sure my boyfriend Kane is well aware of the great woman he has. Thank you for the compliment." I blushed.

"You're more than welcome. I'm going to excuse myself for a moment," he said, leaving my office.

I blew out a breath and picked up a paper to begin fanning myself. I felt the wetness between my legs and felt ashamed that I allowed another man to have me feeling like this. I took another long sip of water from my bottle and had to take some more deep breaths to clear my head. I had to chill out before I drove myself into a panic attack. I quickly went to the restroom and used one of my Summer's Eve wet wipes to wipe away the extra moisture. I made it back to my office before he did.

When he returned, things were more professional, and we were able to finish up our afternoon of shadowing. We agreed that one more day of his observing me should suffice, and he would be ready to try some things out on his own. I had to admit that I enjoyed his company, and the conversation we had in between clients was very stimulating. I could tell that he was very educated as well, and it was nice to interact with someone who wasn't so full of himself. Not that Kane was arrogant, but we were a couple, so we barely discussed anything intellectual.

When the work day came to an end, I almost dreaded leaving because I had to go visit my mother. I loved her dearly, but it tore me up inside to see her in the state she was in. I didn't want her to think she was being a bother, although Kane said that's how I acted. It was very overwhelming to have to look in on her and live my daily life. I wished that car accident had never happened, but it did, and there was nothing I could do about it but continue to move forward like she did. At the end of the day, it was still a hard pill to swallow.

When I pulled up to my mother's house, an eerie feeling came over me. I'm not sure why I felt weird all over but just figured it was a panic attack trying to come on. I quickly went into my purse and popped a Hydroxyzine. I sat in my mother's driveway for a few minutes to see if a calmness would come over me, but for some reason, it wouldn't. I slowly got out of my car and concentrated on controlling my breathing so I wouldn't pass out. As I used my key to let myself, I immediately knew something was wrong.

I walked through my mother's house calling her, but didn't get a response. I panicked and began screaming her name as I ran from room to room looking for her. I searched the house high and low, and my mother was nowhere to be found. I called my brother Alan, but he didn't answer. I called him a couple more times, left a message, and also sent him text messages to call me right away because our mother was missing. I didn't waste any more time and called the police. An officer responded in no time.

He said he normally couldn't take a report until an adult has been missing for at least twenty-four hours, but considering the circumstances with my mother having traumatic brain injury, he felt the need to go ahead and file a report. He said the police department would go ahead issue a Silver Advisory for my mother since she was considered an endangered person. He radioed something in, and the response he got made both of us breath with a sigh of relief.

Ms. Sylvie, the owner of the hair salon down the street, and who had known my mother for years saw her walking near the shop earlier. She had my mother come into the salon and sit down. She had Alan's number and said she called him, but he didn't return her call. She said she was going to bring my mother back home and look for my contact information as soon as she was finished with her client's hair. Meanwhile, she called the non-emergency number to report that my mother was with her in case her family was looking for her. She felt that was important to do since my mother had special needs. I was just glad to know that my mother was safe and that someone cared enough to know that it was unusual for her to be wandering around.

I thanked the officer for coming, and he waited with me while we waited for Ms. Sylvie to bring her home. I was pissed off that Alan still didn't call, but there was no point in me being surprised. He never really was of any

69

help when it came to actually looking after our mother. For years, I had been thinking she shouldn't be living alone in her home and asked her to consider an independent-living facility. She refused, but now I was leaning more toward it. When they walked through the door, I hugged my mother tightly.

"Mama, what were you thinking? Why did you leave?" I asked her.

A confused look came over her face, but then she rubbed my cheek and smiled. "Hi, Almi, baby. I'm so glad you came to see your mama today. You hungry?" she asked.

"No, Mama. Take a seat." I led her over to her comfy chair.

I walked Ms. Sylvie to the front door and thanked her again for looking after my mother. I gave her my telephone number for future use.

"Mama, you know you're not supposed to leave here alone. Something could've happened to you!" I exclaimed.

She scrunched up her face before saying, "Almi,

what are you talking about?"

I looked at her to read her face, and she seemed genuinely confused. I could tell my mother's condition was getting worse, and she really wasn't aware of what just happened. I promise if it wasn't one thing, it was another. I took another deep breath because my stress level suddenly went up a notch.

"Mama, you don't remember just leaving the house? Do you know what just happened?" I asked her slowly.

She just shook her head and looked at me like I was strange. Tears began filling my eyes because it was hurting me to see my mother like this. I couldn't live in denial. Something was going terribly wrong with her, and I needed to make her a doctor's appointment as soon as possible. I also needed to contact the agency who was responsible for her supported-living services and see when the last time a worker was by here helping my mother. I had a feeling they hadn't been around in quite a while.

Chapter 6 Kane

I hung up the phone with Almi as I sat and waited to be called into the conference room for my interview. Almi had just updated me on what the doctor said about her mother having early onset Alzheimer's disease, which was fairly common in someone who suffered a traumatic injury. Her doctor thought it was best to go ahead and place her in a nursing home, because with her health history, he said it wouldn't be long before the disease fully set in. Almi agreed it was best she had twenty-four-hour care, and since she was busy with work and her brother Alan wasn't willing to help that much, she had no choice. I had only met Alan a couple of times, and he seemed a little weird and withdrawn. I thought it was a shame that he wasn't as active in his mother's life as he should be, but that wasn't my place to scold him on that.

Meanwhile, Zavia kept her word on getting me pulled in for an interview. Within a week of me sending her my resume and references, I got a call for an immediate interview. First, Columbia College conducted an interview over the telephone, and now they were bringing me in for a second interview in person. I was excited about the opportunity, and I felt like things were going to go well. I thanked the universe for allowing me to cross paths with Zavia like I did because I was pretty sure I'd still be looking for a job if it wasn't for her. I had to make sure I called her to thank her again later.

"Mr. Williamson?" a middle-aged, bald man, dressed in a navy-blue suit emerged from the office.

"Yes." I confirmed, standing up.

"You ready?" he asked enthusiastically.

"As ready as I'll ever be."

"Then right this way, sir."

I followed him into the conference room where there were three other people sitting behind a long table. They all displayed smiles, which made things less intimidating, so I loosened up some. I spoke my formalities and shook each of their hands before taking a seat.

"Mr. Williamson, you have quite an impressive resume," the bald man spoke.

I was surprised he felt that way, considering the only actual career I ever had was with Dexter Regis. The other two jobs I listed were little mediocre gigs from when I was in undergrad. "Thank you," I replied humbly.

"We're all well aware of the situation with Dexter Regis Technologies, but after our discussion earlier, we really do believe it was an honest mistake. It was a very costly mistake, so I can understand why they felt the need to let you go. However, here at Columbia College, we believe in second chances. It seems you would be a great fit for being a computer-science instructor, that's why we wanted to meet with you. I understand you also had your formal interview over the phone the other day when you spoke with Tangie," the bald man gestured toward one of the women sitting at the table with us.

"Yes, Carl. It was a great pleasure speaking with, Mr. Williamson," Tangie replied to the bald man. "I want you to see this interview as a more informal one. We want to converse with you today and get a feel of who you are."

"That works for me," I replied.

Everyone nodded in agreement, and we did just that. Although they did ask a few interview-like questions, everyone shared laughter and personal stories that were relevant to the questions at hand. By the end of the interview, I felt even more confident about getting the job. As we were wrapping things up, I saw Zavia walk past the window to the conference room and give me the thumbs up. I smiled, but immediately brought my attention back to everyone in the room.

"Well, Mr. Williamson, we normally don't make on-the-spot decisions like this, but I am sure Carl, Janet, and Frank would agree that you are a perfect match for the job," Tangie said. "I would like to extend you a contingent job offer for the position."

"Yes! Thank you! I gladly accept!" I replied excitedly.

"With the exception of what we know happened with Dexter Regis, we still need to run you a criminal background check and a reference check," Tangie informed me.

"That's fine. I know I'll pass with flying colors," I said.

"That shouldn't take too long to do, so I'll just say we'll be in touch by this time next week or sooner if ything comes back before then."

I stood up, shook everyone's hand again, and thanked them for the opportunity. On my way out, I ran into Zavia in the hallway. I scooped her up, spun her in a circle, and gave her a big hug when I put her back down. I could tell I caught her off guard, but she didn't seem to mind.

"I got the job!" I exclaimed.

"Congratulations!" she said, appearing just as excited for me.

"Of course I have to wait for the background check to come back, but otherwise, it's mine."

"See? Aren't you glad you took me up on the suggestion?" She nudged me.

"I'm very glad. I was going to call you later to thank you. I appreciate this. I really do."

"Then we need to celebrate," she said.

"Yeah, we do. I'll call you later so we can get together soon and do that."

"That'll work." She winked before walking away.

I licked my lips and watch her ass bounce in the

tight slacks she wore. I closed my eyes and shook my head. I knew I couldn't allow myself to start getting caught up on this woman. I was in no way going to disrespect Almi. She was all I wanted and needed. What I had with Zavia was a friendship. Nothing more, and nothing less.

I shook my head and blew out a breath as I walked to my car. I looked down, and my dick was standing at attention. When I got in the car, I tried to readjust it and even pinched it to see if it would go down, and nothing. I couldn't get that image of Zavia's juicy ass out of my head. I tried to shift gears by putting my mind on something else, so I decided to call Almi to share the good news.

"Hello?" she answered on the first ring. I could hear sadness in her voice, and I began to hurt for my woman. I hated things weren't going so well with her mother, and at this time, all I wanted to do was comfort her.

"How are you holding up?" I asked her, as if she felt any better than she did when we talked an hour ago.

"I don't know." She sighed. "I'm still trying to process everything. Whether I want to accept it or not, all of this is a part of life's cycle. I wish my mother didn't have to go through all of this, but I know there are people who have gone through worse.

"Well, stay prayerful about things, baby. Everything is going to be OK." I tried to reassure her.

"The reality is, Kane, it's not. I'm not going to try to convince myself that things will be fine when they won't."

I figured there was no point in steady trying to encourage her because one thing I knew about Almi was that when she made up her mind about something, it was a done deal. This was a tough situation, and it seemed like she had a point. Her mother's condition was worsening, and right now, there was no cure for Alzheimer's. I knew there was treatment for it with medications to help manage it but nothing to make it go away. Eventually, it would consume her, especially with the brain injury she previously sustained.

"Well, hopefully, my good news will help elevate your mood just a little," I told her.

"What news?" she continued to sound down and

out.

"I got the job!" I said excitedly. "It's a conditional offer because they still have to run a criminal background check and contact my references, but they already said they knew about the incident with Dexter Regis and weren't going to hold that against me."

"That's nice, Kane. Look, let me call you back," she said, hanging up. I took my phone off my ear and looked at it. I was in total disbelief that she just hung up on me. I was even more hurt that she wasn't as excited as I was. She talked so much about how I wasn't working, but when I told her I was finally about to, she wasn't even supportive. I didn't know what to do to make this lady happy any more. I was close to wanting to just give up, but I wasn't willing to throw away what we had. I knew things would get better once those paychecks started rolling in. I had to cut her a little slack though, because she was going through something right now with her mother. If I was in her shoes, I wouldn't be in a great mood either, so I could give her a pass for her current reaction. I started driving toward the crib, and right as I got a couple of blocks from home, my phone rang. I looked down and saw that it was my father calling. I quickly answered it.

"Hello?"

"Hey, son. Sorry for the spur of the moment, but is right now a good time to meet up with you?" he asked.

"I'm not doing anything, so I guess that will work. Where did you have in mind?"

"Are you hungry? I can sure use a sirloin steak from Texas Roadhouse."

"That's fine with me."

"Is Kirkwood too far for you to get out to?"

"Nah, I can be out there in about thirty minutes I told him."

"That'll work, son. Let me wrap some things up at my office, and I'll meet you out there in about thirty to forty minutes."

I cringed when he said son. He had no right to call me son, and I really don't know why I acknowledged him as my father. I was really trying to be the bigger person here and didn't want to do anything to mess up us being able to establish a bond, so I was going to have to do a lot of biting my tongue this afternoon. I don't know why I didn't tell Almi my father had reached out to me. I guess because I didn't know what would really become of it, so I was keeping it to myself. I would tell her soon enough, when I felt like things would go well and not just be a temporary thing. Meanwhile, I text messaged her telling her I love her and would be home a little later.

By the time I pulled into the Texas Roadhouse in Kirkwood, I noticed that Almi never replied. I wasn't going to stress over it but allow her the space she needed for the moment. I called my father back to see if he was here or close by, and he said he was getting off Interstate 44, which was only a couple of minutes away. I decided to wait in the car so we could walk in together.

It was an awkward moment when he pulled up, because I hesitated to get out of the car. I saw him step out of a charcoal-gray Maserati Levante and look around as if he were looking for me. He pulled out his phone and within seconds, my phone began ringing. I rejected his call, took a deep breath, and stepped from my car. I drove a 2017 Infiniti Q50. One of Almi's clients hooked her up on a great deal for a car, so I paid the man a visit for myself. He struck me the same deal as Almi, but we both agreed to tell her I only got 25%, versus the same 75% he gave her. Why we weren't truthful? I can't really say. I guess it was a man thing. A man still wanted to feel like a man and in control of things. It bruised our egos a little bit for others to know we received a little charity.

    I cleared my throat, and my father looked my way. A smile came across his face, but I continued to wear a blank expression on mine. I was completely emotionless. Although I had seen pictures of him online, now that we were face-to-face, I studied his features a little more and could actually see quite a resemblance. I was sure my mother saw it a lot too, but since she never liked to speak of my father, she refused to say it. My mother still lived back in Kansas City, and we spoke often. However, I never told her anything about speaking with my father because I knew she wouldn't be pleased.

    We walked into the restaurant together and were seated right away. As if reading my mind, he asked me how my mother was doing. I gave him a look that said it all, and he left the subject alone. I don't know where my boldness went because I usually wasn't one not to speak my mind, but I didn't want to blow up at him on our first visit with each other. Besides, I had already told myself that although I was angry on the inside, I was going to be mature and conduct myself like an adult.

He insisted I ordered anything I wanted since he was paying. I did just that, ordering a Fort Worth ribeye with a side of broccoli and a loaded baked potato. I ordered a Bud Light Lime as well. My father ordered the USDA choice sirloin steak with corn, green beans, and a water. I guess he was keeping it simple today and not as extra as I thought a man of his caliber would have been.

"So why did you really want to meet?" I asked, while we waited for our food to arrive.

"I told you, to get to know you," he replied, sipping his water.

"Why after all these years?" I inquired. I told myself I wasn't going to do this, but I had to know.

"I looked for you a couple of times before and even kept tabs on you. You seemed to be doing well, and I didn't want to interrupt your life. When I saw on the news what happened with Dexter Regis Technologies, I figured I should reach out to you and see if I could be of any assistance. I waited because I wanted to give you your space for a while and not come on too strong."

"I actually just received a conditional offer for a job today right before you called. They know about what happened with the technology company. I'm just waiting for them to receive my criminal background check," I told him.

"I'm glad to hear that. Where will you be working?"

"I'll be working as a computer-science instructor at Columbia College," I told him.

"That seems like a *reputable* career," he said. I could sense him throwing a little shade.

"Yeah, it's an honest living versus me being out here selling dope or robbing hardworking people," I said.

"I agree. Have you considered any type of sales work or real estate?" he asked.

"Why? You offering me a position in your

business?" I asked him.

"That can be worked out if you're interested. I was just curious about what else it is you're good at or what else you may have considered."

"I also have an interest in gaming. The whole computer thing is pretty much my entire life."

"I understand."

Our food arrived, and we continued to make small talk. I guess this was his idea of getting to know each other. It was nice to know that if I had not gotten the job today, I may have been able to fall back on my father to help with finding some work. I still think it's weird he decided to resurface, even though he gave that cheesy ass reason. I wanted to stay in his good graces though, because I was determined to get added to his will or left some part of his riches. I felt that was the least bit he could do in his years of absence. I still felt like there was something more about him coming into my life all of a sudden, and I was determined to find out.

Chapter 7 Almi

Things in my life just seemed to go from bad to worse. The holidays came and went. My mother was becoming more ill by the day. Kane started working a couple of months ago, right after the New Year, and I thought things were going to get better, but they haven't. He seemed even more distant now, and he was always busy. On Valentine's Day, he gave me a single rose, a box of chocolates, and left a card next to it telling me he'd be working late. It was great that he was able to help with the bills again, and we were in a better position financially, but our relationship seemed like it went from bad to worse. I got tired of trying to plead with him for time and attention, so I've been giving all the extra time I have to my mother.

I sat with her by her bedside holding her hand while she slept peacefully. I used my other hand to wipe away the tears that were falling from my eyes. I didn't understand why life had to be so hard. It seemed nothing could ever go smoothly, but I was always fighting some type of battle. The last person I thought I'd have to fight with would be Kane. He was supposed to be my helpmate, but instead, he was becoming my enemy. He never gave me a reason not to trust him, but my gut instinct had been telling me that something wasn't right. I loved this man with my all, and I wanted things to work out for us. I was hoping this was only a rough patch for now and that things would be alright for us in the long run.

"Mama?" I whispered, not really wanting to wake her. I needed to let her know I was going to be leaving. I came by to see her on my lunch break and would be back later after I got off work.

"Hmm?" she moaned, barely stirring awake.

"I have to go now. I will be back later," I told her.

She never opened her eyes but just smiled. I was satisfied with that and kissed her forehead. The tears began falling again, and I quickly wiped them before stepping out of her room. I waved goodbye to the nursing staff and told them I'd be back after work. This had become my routine, so they pretty much knew to expect me. I liked to have dinner with my mama, so they would hold off on bringing her dinner until after I had arrived.

When I sat in my car, I could no longer hold the

tears but cried a river. I felt my shoulders heaving, and I let out a sob, because all of this hurt so bad. It felt like the weight of the world was on my shoulders. I was in this alone, and it made me resent my brother Alan even more. He acted like he didn't have a care in the world. How could someone do their mother like that? She was a damn good mother to us before the car accident, so I wasn't sure why he closed her out like he did. All these years, I wondered if it was just his way of dealing with the pain by not facing it, or if it really was him just being plain-old selfish. There were times I felt overwhelmed and didn't want to be bothered, but I never completely shut her out like he did.

I allowed myself to continue crying as I drove back to work. When I pulled into the parking lot, I knew I had to get myself together before I stepped foot into the building. I cleaned my face and reapplied my makeup before I got out of my car. I held my head high and sashayed into the building with a forced smile on my face.

"Good afternoon, Misha." I spoke to our afternoon receptionist.

"How are you today, Almi?" She smiled back at

me. "Are you ready for me to forward your calls back to your office?"

"Give me about fifteen minutes to settle in, then go right ahead," I told her.

She nodded as she took a call that was coming into the switchboard. I went to the break room to fix myself some coffee and bumped into Marshall and one of our co-workers, Winnie. She was laughing in Marshall's face and even did one of those moves where she patted her voluptuous breast for him to notice. I never really cared for her much, and for some reason, the laughter they shared made me a little jealous. I had become so used to Marshall giving me a lot of attention that it was weird to see him laughing with someone else. I really needed to get my feelings in check because I was tripping. It's not like he was my man, and even if he were, there was nothing wrong with sharing a laugh with someone else.

"Good afternoon, Marshall. Hello, Winnie." I spoke to the both of them.

"Hey, girl!" Winnie said cheerfully and winked at Marshall as she walked out the break room.

He chuckled and shook his head before speaking back to me. "Good afternoon, beautiful."

"Humph. Beautiful? How do I know you didn't just say that to her?" I replied offensively.

"Whoa. Wait a minute." Marshall threw up his hands in defense. "Where did that come from?"

"I mean, she *was* just giggling all up in your face. I assume you must use that *beautiful* line with all the ladies around here," I snapped.

"No. Only you," he said, raising his eyebrow. "Why are you so upset? It's not like you're my lady, but you're acting a little jealous like you are. What's going on with you today?"

"Don't flatter yourself, Marshall. I'm well aware of the fact that I'm not your woman, and believe me, I'm not trying to be. I have a man, remember?"

"Well, act like it. You shouldn't be stressing over who I'm calling beautiful, but I can assure you that it's only you," he said, pulling me close to him in a bold move.

I looked him in eyes, and he looked me right back in mine. I felt the heat between us, and our faces were moving in closer for a kiss. Winnie walked back into the break room, interrupting our moment, and we jumped back from each other. I cleared my throat before I grabbed my cup of coffee and walked out. I didn't bother to look Winnie in her face. I didn't want to see her facial expression. I was actually grateful for the interruption before I had the chance to commit my first act of infidelity. I had been faithful to Kane our entire relationship, and although we were experiencing hard times right now, I didn't want to do anything to jeopardize what we had.

The rest of my work day went by in a blur, because I couldn't stop thinking about Marshall and the intimate moment we shared. I was ashamed of myself for letting things go that far, and I didn't know how I was going to face him going forward. There were definitely some type of chemistry between us. We did spend our lunch breaks together whether in the office or out at a restaurant. I was beginning to think of him more as a friend than just a co-worker. It's not like it was love though, because we've only known each other for a few weeks and only interacted during work hours. I still didn't know why I acted jealous earlier either, but for some reason, seeing him close to Winnie like that made me feel some type of way. I enjoyed the attention he gave me, since Kane had been slacking, and maybe it was the fact that I didn't want to share that attention.

As soon as five o'clock came, I flew out of my office so I could get back to the nursing home. They served beef stew tonight, and it wasn't too bad. My mama said she could make hers better, and we shared a few laughs. She had a couple of moments of confusion, but we made it through our meal with few incidents. I stayed while the nurse took her vitals and while the doctor came in to look her over. He said he had some more tests to run on her in the upcoming days and that he would keep me posted. I thanked the staff before leaving and heading home.

When I arrived home, I was surprised to see Kane was there. He was so consumed with this new job and hanging out lately that we barely saw each other anymore. He was moving around the kitchen, setting the table for dinner. I smiled, happy to see that we would finally be getting a chance to spend some time together.

"What did you cook?" I asked him, setting my work bag and purse down on the counter.

"Would you mind taking that into the bedroom? We have a guest arriving in a few," he said.

I was a little disappointed because it wasn't going to be any alone time for us after all. He wasn't fixing dinner for me; he was making dinner for whoever we were expecting. I felt stupid for getting excited for nothing. I was also perturbed he asked me to put my things away. I always set them on the counter before with no issue. He was really trying to impress someone this evening. I did as he asked though, and when I went back into the kitchen, I tried to kiss him, but he moved away. That shit hurt even more.

"Hold on, bae. Let me get this food right quick," he said, moving over to the pot and stirring away.

"I'm not really that hungry," I told him. "You know I had dinner with my mother this evening, like I always do."

"Well, can you at least try to nibble at something and not ruin things for me tonight?" he asked a bit annoyed.

"Ruin things? Who exactly are we expecting tonight?"

"It's a surprise. You'll see in a minute," he said, finally kissing me.

It was almost like it was forced kiss. Rough, quick, and wet. It grossed me out a little, but I figured I had better be happy to be getting that much from him, considering the way things had been going lately.

"What are you making?" I asked, showing a little interest. I had to admit he had it smelling good.

"I'm making white-chicken chili, garlic-cheddar biscuits, and a Caesar salad," he said.

"That actually sounds good." I complimented him.

"I know," he said a little bit too arrogantly for me. I shrugged it off, because maybe I was being extra sensitive for no reason right now, and he didn't mean it in a rude way at all.

"I've never seen you go all out for anyone like this but me. This person must be really special, huh?"

"I guess you can say that."

"Is your mom in town?" I asked excitedly, realizing that's who it must be.

"I wish. You know she refuses to step foot into St. Louis since…" His voice trailed off.

I should have known better than to ask. He was right. His mother refused to come to St. Louis because of the hate she had for Kane's father and how she said he embarrassed her when she told him she was pregnant. She made the announcement one Christmas in front of her friends and family. He had fed her these stories about how much he loved her and would marry her one day, but when she told him she was pregnant, he denied their child and left her standing there. She was so humiliated that she left for Kansas City, Missouri the next day and never looked back. The only time we saw her was when we went up there and the one time we took her to Williamsburg, Virginia to Busch Gardens on vacation a couple of summers ago. She wouldn't even come to St. Louis for her family reunions because she still harbored the shame of that day. Kane never got to know any of his family except for his mother and one of his mother's sisters who would come visit them over the years. She didn't have any children though, so he didn't even know any of his cousins. I really think that's why he came to St. Louis for college to get acquainted with his roots, but he never did, just so he wouldn't upset his mother.

I continued to watch him move around the kitchen with precision, really focused on the task at hand. Since he wasn't going to tell me who was coming, I had no choice but to wait. He finally looked up at me when he noticed me watching him and crinkled his eyebrow.

"Are you going to change clothes?" he asked.

"What's wrong with what I have on?" I wondered.

"I just thought you may want to put on something nicer," he said.

"Excuse you!" I exclaimed, really hurt by that blow. I dressed up for work every day, so I automatically looked nice Monday through Friday. He had a lot of fucking nerve right now.

"I mean, we are expecting guests, and I figured you wouldn't want to prance around in your work clothes."

"You know what, Kane? I am not about to go there

with you right now," I said, walking away from him. I was truly at a loss for words right now. I really didn't know who this man was anymore. It's like he didn't have a care in the world for anyone but himself. He used to be so careful with me, but now, he came off so nonchalant and conceited about things. A few minutes ago, I thought I was tripping, but now I think he was the one who lost his damn noodles.

I don't know why I even listened to him, but I went ahead to change clothes for argument's sake. I wanted to get more comfortable anyway. I picked out some more slacks and a simple blouse but opted for some flats instead of my stilettos. I touched up my makeup for the thousandth time today and bumped my hair a little with the flat iron. When I was satisfied with my look, I reemerged from the bedroom. Kane gave me his approval with a smile and nod. He walked up to me to kiss me, but I turned my head, so that the kiss landed on my cheek. He shrugged, and I took a seat on the sofa.

"So how was your day?" he finally asked, after all this time.

"Fine," I gave him a one word reply.

"What's wrong with you now? Please don't ruin our dinner with your attitude," he begged.

I cut my eyes at him, rolled them hard, and looked back at the television without even satisfying him with a reply. The doorbell rang a few minutes later, piquing my interest. I would finally get to see who the hell this mystery person was that had Kane tripping all over himself. This person better be worth it too. He answered the door, and in walked a middle-aged man who greeted him with a handshake. I immediately saw the resemblance but also thought the man coming into our home looked familiar.

"Well, this absolutely stunning young lady here must be Almi," the man said.

"Why, yes I am," I replied with a fake smile, doing my best to seem polite. I still didn't know what the hell was going on, but I was anxiously awaiting confirmation.

"Almi, this is my father, Wesley Clayton," Kane said excitedly.

I knew I recognized him. This man's face was plastered on the sides of buses and billboards all across town. He was a very wealthy man who owned and managed a lot of properties in St. Louis. It's strange I never noticed how much Kane and Mr. Clayton looked alike until now. What the hell made him resurface after all these years, especially after he denied his son? What made him so accepting of Kane all of a sudden? I was really good at following my gut instincts, and something told me that this man had some ill intentions. I didn't feel good about him being in our presence at this moment. I guess he could sense how I was feeling, because he looked at me uncomfortably before turning his attention back to Kane.

"So what did you prepare for dinner for us this evening?" Mr. Clayton asked.

Kane repeated the exact same menu he repeated to me while taking some of my Caymus Cabernet wine out the cabinet. I gave him a look of disapproval, silently telling him to put my good shit back. He had better reach up there and grab some damn Boone's Farm or Sutter Home. The expensive wine was for me and me only. He was lucky I even shared with him every once in a while. He ignored the face I was making and continued to make small talk with his father. I blew out a breath rather loudly, drawing both of their attention.

"So what is it that you do for a living?" Mr. Clayton asked me, taking a seat at the kitchen table.

I swear I wanted to say something smart, but I caught myself. I was trying to be on my best behavior, but it was hard as hell to right now. "I'm a senior accountant at—" I was in the middle of answering his question before I was cut off by the doorbell. "We're expecting more guests?"

"Yes. I hope you all don't mind that I invited my daughter as well. Kane, I wanted you to meet your sister," Mr. Clayton said.

Who the fuck did he think he was to make an appearance in my home like he was God and then to invite someone along with him? I had a few choice words for Kane about his so-called father when this visit was over.

"I have a sister?" Kane asked with even more excitement.

"Yes. I wanted to surprise you. I think it's time we all get to know each other better." He confirmed.

"Humph, so now he all of a sudden wants to get to know you. I bet he knew your *sister* all this time," I mumbled under my breath.

"What was that you said, bae?" Kane asked.

"Nothing." I sighed, forcing another fake smile, as I went to the door to answer.

My heart dropped to my stomach when I saw who was looking back at me. The smile disappeared off her face too. You have to be fucking kidding me. Of all the people in the world, my co-worker Winnie was his sister.

Chapter 8 Kane

"Thank you for coming out with me tonight and having a drink," I said to Zavia.

"No problem. We both need a stress reliever after midterms," she said.

We were back at Classics, and Lord knows I needed to unwind. It has been quite hectic this week, but I was glad midterm testing had finally come to an end. It reminded me of back when I was in college, because that same stress was all over my students' faces. I was tired of them coming to me asking for extra credit if they failed their tests. I assured them midterms were not as big of a deal as they thought, and I wasn't going to use it to factor their overall grade. Some weren't convinced, and the fact that they stressed made me stress. I don't see how the hell one could fail a computer-science class anyway.

Almi said she was going to stay at the nursing home with her mother a little longer after they had dinner. I knew she had to be there for her mother, but things were a bit frustrating because it seemed like we no longer spent time. Our sex life was now non-existent. When I wanted to spend time, she was busy, and vice versa. I don't know what was happening to us, but it wasn't looking too good. I wanted to talk to her about it, but I almost felt like it was a lost cause. Perry was living out of town now, so I couldn't vent to him about it. Buffalo was always busy with his wife—the way I would like things to be with Almi. Raynell was still busy playing the field, so he wouldn't be able to give me any sound advice. The only other person I could think of was Zavia. We had grown a lot more closer since we were co-workers now, and I really valued our friendship.

"A penny for your thoughts," she said, bringing me back to the here and now.

I almost quoted Usher and said a nickel for your kiss, but caught myself. "There are just some things on my mind about me and Almi's relationship," I told her.

"A little trouble in paradise, huh? Tell me about it," she said.

I took a deep breath before I began speaking. "I thought things were going to get better between me and Almi once I started working, but it seems to have gotten worse. We're back on track financially, but our time together is now few and far in between. I spend a lot of time at the college with the students, and she spends a lot of time at the nursing home with her ill mother. By the time we both make it home in the evenings, we're both tired. Weekends are no better, because I'm grading assignments and then trying to get a little me time to unwind from a rough week. We seem to have lost our connection, and I'm not even going to bother talking about sex."

"You might want to talk with her about how you feel before it gets even more worse. You both have physical and emotional needs that need to be addressed. You don't want to keep putting this off because it can be even more detrimental to your relationship. Continuing to ignore each other's needs and go down this same path will be what ultimately ruins you two," she replied knowingly.

"You seem to have a lot of expertise on this topic."

"I'm only telling you from experience. Been there, done that already."

"I want to fix it, but I don't know if she really wants to anymore."

"How can you know if you don't bring your concerns to her. Both of you are still currently in it for the moment. If no one has left yet, talked about leaving yet, or made any moves to leave, then things can be worked out."

"I sure hope so." I sighed.

"I know so," she said with a smile.

Zavia was so easy to talk to. We continued to converse and crack jokes about a few things that had been going on at work. We even had a little joning session going. I was in good spirits when I was around her, and it was different from being with Almi. I loved Almi a lot, but we lacked fun in our relationship. Things used to be fun in the beginning, but not anymore. I wished I could swap Zavia's personality for Almi's. I knew it was a weird concept, but if there was a way to combine them, I would.

"I'm getting a little sleepy. I'm going to call it a night." Zavia yawned.

Yawning was contagious, so that triggered a yawn for me as well. "I feel you. What are you about to get into?" I asked her.

"The bed. I just said I was tired." She nudged me

playfully.

"Yeah, you did." I laughed. "What are you doing tomorrow?"

"Since when have you been interested in my activities?" she asked, raising her eyebrows.

"I don't know. I'm just trying to make a little small talk. I'm not quite ready for the night to end. If I had to take a wild guess, I could bet you a $100 that Almi is still not home. I'll be bored tonight until I lie down and fall asleep."

"Fine, Kane. I can stay about another hour, but that's it. I'm ready to go home and take a shower," she said.

"I'm not asking you to stay. Go ahead and handle your business. I'll have another drink before I head out."

"No. You've had enough. You're still sober enough for now. I definitely don't want you getting tipsy. In my opinion, tipsy is still drunk, and therefore, you won't need to be behind the wheel once you get to that point. I wouldn't be able to live with myself if anything happened to you."

"At least you care. It seems that between you, my

father, and sister, that's about it."

"Oh, hush. Almi cares about you. I know your mother does because you've said nothing but great things about her. Your friend Perry you told me about I'm sure cares about you as well."

"My mother and Perry don't count right now because they're not local at this point."

"Boy, hush. You be safe, and I'll see you at work tomorrow." Zavia got up and kissed me on the cheek.

I sighed. "See you tomorrow."

She walked to the door but then abruptly turned around and came back. Reading her facial expression, I could tell she was nervous about what she was about to say. She came back, rubbed her hand over the back of my head, and kissed my forehead before she spoke. "Kane, I'm really concerned about you, and I feel like you could use a friend right now. This is going to go against all my values, and I've been careful to stay in my place thus far, but I'm going to ask anyway. Do you want to come over for a little while so you won't be so lonely tonight?"

"How would that be going against your values?

We're friends. It's not like we would do anything we're not supposed to," I told her.

"I haven't wanted to cross that line with you because I respect what you have with Almi. However, I just feel like you could really use some support right now. Like I said, I'm just not comfortable leaving you at the bar to drink yourself to death. At least I can sleep tonight if I'm not concerned about how much you'll sit here and drink. I can brew a pot of coffee while I take a shower, and we can sit up and chat some more for a while. Nothing more, nothing less."

"That sounds fine to me," I told her.

"Great, now follow me," she said, taking my hand and pulling me off the bar stool.

I followed her like a long, lost, sick puppy, not knowing my life was about to change forever.

***

"Kane, we don't have to do this." Zavia panted in between breaths. Things had just gotten hot and heavy between us as we sat on her couch. I can't really tell you who came on to who, because we both had been drinking.

So much for that pot of coffee. She pulled out a bottle of Cîroc and glasses no sooner than we got there. I knew I had to take responsibility for what was about to happen next, because I could have just walked way, but I didn't.

Instead of replying, I stuck my tongue back down Zavia's throat. I was so sexually frustrated because Almi hadn't been fulfilling her role as my woman. I told myself for so long I wasn't going to cross that line with Zavia, but I was a man with needs. I promised myself this was going to be a one-time thing and never cheat on her again. I figured every man was entitled to that one mistake in a relationship, as long as they didn't let it happen again. I kept trying to convince myself that Almi pushed me to do this because she had been rejecting me.

I helped Zavia lift her shirt and bra over her head. Her beautiful D-cup breasts stood perky and begged me to suck them. I did just that, sucking on one and massaging the other nipple between my thumb and forefinger. She let out a sexy moan, and I rotated titties. I ran my hand over her body, enjoying how soft and thick she was. Don't get me wrong, Almi was a brick house too, but this woman had a different look and different smell. Sometimes we all needed something different every once in a while. I was now starting to see why Raynell bounced from woman to woman. He probably got bored easily. It wasn't my interest to do that though. I loved Almi dearly. I just wanted to fulfill my immediate need in the moment. In order to do that, I had to push all thoughts of Almi out of my head and focus on the goddess I had before me.

    I continued to lick and kiss all over Zavia's body. I felt her hands move across my chiseled chest, down my stomach, until she released my dick from my pants. She stroked him back to life, considering I started going a little soft when I thought about Almi a few moments ago. Her hand felt warm around my dick, and the excitement of being with Zavia forced a moan to escape from my lips. I hadn't even penetrated her yet, and this woman had already captured my soul.

    We made our way to her bedroom, and I knew there was no turning back. For the hundredth time, I had to push thoughts of Almi out of my head if I wanted to go through with this. Zavia lay her naked body down on the bed and looked up at me with eyes pleading for me to take her to another level. I did just that as I gently pushed her legs back and took in her beautifully shaven mound. I inhaled her aroma, and the scent of her juices danced in my nostrils. My lips connected with her perfect set of pussy lips as I planted kisses on them and gently stroked my tongue across her swollen clitoris.

    Her back arched as I began to eat away greedily, as if her dripping pussy would be my last meal. Her moans made me go harder and faster as I flicked my tongue and bounced it against her pearl. I licked and sucked away, and as her excitement increased, so did mine. I was determined to bring her to a climax, and I did just that as she began jerking and bucking her body against my face. Completely satisfied at accomplishing my goal, I came up for air and slowly eased my muscle into her wet spot. I stroked her long but hard as I looked into her eyes. This woman was beyond beautiful, even while making ugly faces filled with pains of pleasure. I kissed her, and she licked her juices from around my lips and chin hairs, and that shit drove me wild.

We kept a nice rhythm going, and I had to coach myself to keep my nut down. I wasn't ready to bust yet, at least not until I felt her cum down my dick. With that in mind, I rolled on my back and pulled her on top of me. She rode my dick like a madwoman, and I enjoyed every bit of it. When she started squatting over the dick and I lifted my head to watch it go in and out of her, I completely lost it. I gripped her waist tight and began guiding her body. That nut was rising to the tip of my dick, and I didn't know how much longer I could hold out. I could tell she was growing tired of squatting, and she sat back down on it. As she rocked back and forth, I had her lean forward so I could suck her nipples. Her intense moans told me she was about to cum, and that made me release my nut into her as I felt her pussy pulsate around my dick.

    She kissed my lips before she climbed off of me. She laid down next to me, and I pulled her close into a spooning position. I inhaled the scent of her hair and smiled. For now, I was going to continue enjoying the moment before I had to face reality. I knew I would have to be careful not to wear the guilt on my face but just go with the flow of things when I came face-to-face with Almi. As good as the sex just was with Zavia, this was it. Too bad I couldn't call it a one-night stand. The only tricky thing about this was moving forward at work and in this friendship with Zavia without allowing it to make us change. I closed my eyes and got lost in my thoughts.

Chapter 9 Almi

When I woke up this morning, I looked at Kane with disgust. He was curled up like a little baby with no care in the world. It was Friday, and he only had one late-morning class he taught, so he got to sleep in late. I fell asleep early last night but woke up when I felt him get into the bed next to me. I glanced at the clock on the nightstand, and it was after one a.m. when he came in. I was in no mood to argue, so I just rolled my eyes and went back to sleep. We needed to have a talk about him going out with his boys so much. This was starting to get played out, and we needed to figure something out to bring us back to the point where we used to be.

For now, I was still frustrated with him, so I quickly got ready for work and did my best not to make too much noise to wake him. He stirred a couple of times, and I froze into place. I don't know why. I just wasn't ready to face him this morning. I needed more time to think, and by the end of my workday, I would know exactly how I wanted to approach things with him. Meanwhile, I decided to make a slight change in my day, especially considering I was caught up with things at work for now. I wanted to stop by the nursing home this morning before work, so I could be present for the annual appreciation lunch my boss did for the employees every year.

When I arrived at the nursing home, my mother was sitting in a chair, looking at the television. She wasn't watching it because it was off, but she stared at the screen as if she were watching something. I shook my head because I hated to know that my mother's health was still getting worse.

"Hey, Ma," I said, coming into her room and setting my coat down on her bed. I leaned in to give her a kiss, but a confused look came across her face, and she leaned back to dodge my greeting.

"Who are you?" she asked.

I closed my eyes as tears began welling in my eyes. "It's me, Mama. I'm Almi," I told her.

"Oh, hey, Almi baby." She smiled, finally allowing me to kiss her. "How are you this evening?"

"It's still morning time, Mama. Did you eat any breakfast yet?"

She waved her hand and folded her arms. "They said they have to start giving me baby food because I've been choking off my food lately."

"Well, Ma, you did choke a couple of times the last couple of days. It's not baby food though. They're just putting it a blender or food processor, adding a little liquid, and pureeing it. It might be safer to make sure you don't keep choking." I tried to convince her.

"I'm not eating no damn baby food. To hell with them people, and to hell with you if you agree with them," she said.

"Aw, Mama. It's going to be OK. Did you want some applesauce or pudding with your breakfast?" I asked, still trying to convince her she needed to eat something.

"I said I'm not eating any of that mess they're trying to serve me," she said.

"Mama, you gotta eat something. You have to keep up your strength," I told her.

She turned back toward the television and started staring at it again as if I weren't there. I didn't understand how things seemed to keep going from bad to worse day after day. I've heard of some people living with Alzheimer's for a few years before it completely took over, but my mother barely had this diagnosis for a few months. I wasn't even sure what stage she was in. I needed to speak with the doctor about what was going on.

I stepped into the hallway to see if I could spot a medical staff member walking by. When I finally got a nurse's attention, she assured me she would have the doctor come in as soon as he finished his rounds. I sat and watched my mother stare off into space. She seemed to make a couple of involuntary movements and jerks with her body, but I shrugged it off.

"Good morning, Mrs. Prentiss. How are you feeling today?" the doctor came in and spoke to my mother. She looked at him strangely and went back to staring at the television again.

"Hello, Dr. Ackerman. Any news?" I asked him.

"Good morning to you as well, Ms. Almi," Dr. Ackerman acknowledged me. "I'm afraid that we actually need to order some more tests. I noticed some rather unusual things, and I'm sure you would agree when I say it seems like she's moving through the stages of Alzheimer's a little too quickly. I'm afraid something else may be going on."

"That's actually why I called for you to come in here because I thought so too. Just a few minutes ago, it seemed like she was making some random movements as well. I never noticed them before."

"What kind of movements?"

"Kind of like twitching and jerking movements."

"Ah… I see," he said, writing something down on his notepad. I am going to get her in for testing right away. I promise to let you know something as soon as we have more answers," he said.

He tried to take a few vitals, but my mother refused to cooperate. He didn't force her, but said he'd have her nurse try again a little later. I thanked him as I always did and just sat there holding her hand for a little while longer. After about twenty minutes, I decided to pull away because I needed to get to work. I almost regretted choosing the employee luncheon over coming to sit with my mother like I always did, but I knew it was important to still build in some time for myself. Unfortunately, Kane was still on some other mess, so I found pleasure in things like lunch with my co-workers.

I hit Interstate 270 South to head to work. I connected my phone to the Bluetooth in my car and found my R&B playlist. I turned the speakers all the way to maximum volume when Dru Hill "These Are The Times" came on. It made me reminisce back to the good times Kane and I shared. I needed him more than ever right now. I really don't know what happened to us, but we needed to get that strength and love back into our relationship. I know I haven't been the easiest person to deal with these past few months with my mother's illness and my mood swings, but he should know to charge it to my head and not my heart. I thought he would have tried a little harder to console me and work through the motions with me, but I was wrong. I guess I was partly responsible for pushing him away, considering all I did was nag when he didn't have a job. Being realistic though, what woman wouldn't get frustrated with her man not working? At this point, we were going to have to put the bad days behind us and begin moving forward with better days.

When I got to work, I headed straight for the break room like I always did and poured myself a cup of coffee. Although I know she didn't care to, Winnie came in and spoke, so I spoke back. I felt her eyeballing me, but I didn't bother to feed in to her shenanigans. Once I learned that she was Kane's sister, there had been even more tension between us. We were never really friends or anything before then, just co-workers who were cordial. Well, things seemed to change a little, and I think it had a lot to do with her having a thing for Marshall, who wouldn't give her the time of day. Marshall continued trying to shoot his shot with me, but I just wasn't the type to try juggling two men. He knew I was taken, and so did I; therefore, I never let this office romance he kept striving for actually take off. Don't get me wrong, I was attracted to him. He made my body react in strange ways whenever he was around. I just knew it would be wrong to even slightly entertain him, so I left well enough alone.

The night I met their father and Winnie joined us for dinner was quite awkward. She seemed to smirk at me a lot and throw around subliminal statements, but I always had a comeback for her before she finally gave up altogether. The next day, she told me to watch myself because she sees how Marshall and I flirt with each other. She threatened to tell her brother, but she didn't have anything to tell him. Yeah, she walked in on Marshall and I almost kissing, but that was it. Anything could have been taking place, and since she didn't have ocular proof otherwise, what she *thought* didn't matter.

I was in my office for barely five complete minutes before Marshall showed up at my door. I was in the middle of listening to messages, so I signaled for him to come in and close the door behind him. I gave him a soft smile and nodded at him as he took a seat. I had a few things I wanted to talk with him about anyway, including one of the accounts he messed up on. I jotted down a couple of people I needed to call back before lunch and turned my attention to Marshall.

"I'm glad you came by here. We need to talk about Kayson McPeters's account." I raised my eyebrow.

He threw his head back, already knowing what I

was talking about, and blew out a breath. He folded his hands behind his head and stared at me intently, obviously waiting for me to finish. We had a staring competition for a few more seconds because I was waiting for his explanation. Even though he's been here for a few months, he was still considered the new guy, and his accounts still came across my desk for final approval on some things.

He finally let out a chuckle and said, "Look, Almi. I know I messed up on that account. I was adding numbers too fast, put some extra numbers in, but I did try to go back and fix it."

"So why didn't you just ask for help? What you did almost looked fraudulent like you and Mr. McPeters concocted a little scheme against the boss or something. Thankfully, I caught the error and was able to straighten it out."

"I appreciate that. I just figured I'm supposed to have things together by now, not still make silly errors. I was embarrassed to ask for help."

"Well, your embarrassment could have costed your job and our company that account. Don't be ashamed.

We're human, and we all make mistakes every once in a while. It's your first mistake, that I noticed anyway, since you've been with us. I still make mistakes too. Next time, if you're not really sure how to fix it, please come ask me. I wanted to come to you versus letting our boss or anyone else know. It's fixed, and now we can move on," I told him.

"Thank you again, Almi," he said.

"No problem," I replied.

I smiled and was about to pick up the phone on my desk to make a call, but I noticed Marshall staring at me deeply like he always did. He sent a shiver up my spine, but I had to control the situation and not let this man continue to get to me in ways that he didn't even know. "What? Is there something on my face?" I asked him.

"No. Not at all. I know I've told you time and time again, but Almi, you are just so beautiful. You come to work every day with a smile, but behind that smile, I can tell you mask so much pain. Why don't you ever talk to me?"

"I prefer to separate my work life and personal life. There's nothing to really talk about."

"I consider us friends, and a friend can tell when another one is in need of comfort. I'm all ears. Get it off your chest."

He had caught me off guard, because I could no longer front with the persona I had been trying to uphold. He was absolutely right. I had so much mess on my plate that it was consuming me, and I was on the verge of a mental breakdown. I took a deep breath and told him everything from my mother's illness, my brother not helping with anything, and the issues I had been having with Kane. I even took it further and told him about Winnie being Kane's sister and how she threatened to tell him that something was going with us. I probably should have told him that part a long time ago, but like I said, I kept personal issues separate from my work life.

I was a mess by the time I got everything off my chest, and I couldn't stop the tears from flowing. It seemed like all I ever did was cry lately. I would give anything for a moment of peace and happiness, but that didn't seem to be what the universe had in store for me at the moment.

Out of nowhere, the room started spinning, and I

began hyperventilating. I became hot all over, and my heart was beating out of my chest. I closed my eyes and placed my hands flat against my desk, trying to will away the panic attack I was having.

"Almi! Almi! Are you OK?" I heard Marshall ask, but he sounded so far away. It was almost like he was shouting my name through a tunnel.

I opened my eyes and signaled for him to go the cabinet. He did as I needed him to do, and I was barely able to instruct him to hand me my purse from out of there. It took a couple of tries, but he got the message and was able to look inside and grab my prescription pills. I hurriedly popped my medicine, gulped down some water, and sat back, waiting for it work. Marshall sat across from me, looking at me with so much concern in his eyes. After a few minutes, I felt better.

"I'm sorry," I said to him, forcing a smile.

"What are you sorry for? That's the reason you needed to get that off your chest. At least you didn't have a panic attack while driving or out in public somewhere. My sister has anxiety disorder, so I know firsthand how sometimes those attacks can be hard to control."

"I don't have anxiety disorder. Sometimes I just have panic attacks. It's nothing."

"Same difference. Besides, you just popped a damn pill for it. Obviously, you were diagnosed. There is nothing to be ashamed of. You're human. We all have imperfections."

"Marshall. I'm fine. Really."

"That's the problem with you, Almi! You act like your life is so put together. You just sat here and told me everything going on with you, and yes, that is a shitload of stuff to carry. Why do you always have to act like you're superwoman instead of admitting that sometimes you need someone to be there for you? Let me be that person and be there for you. I know you have a man, but obviously, he's not stepping up and doing his part in making sure you're OK. Yeah, he got the whole financial thing going for himself again, but a woman has to be taken care of mentally and emotionally as well. When are you going to realize your worth?"

"Marsh—"

"No, answer me. When will you stop long enough to know your worth and understand that it's OK to need someone to lean on for support?"

I could see he was not going to drop the subject, so I looked down at my hands. I shook my head and bit down on my bottom lip to keep the tears from falling again. I hated for this man to see me so vulnerable like this. I was a strong woman. I had to carry myself as a strong woman.

"Marshall, I appreciate you. I really do. You're right. I needed to get those things off my chest, but I'm fine now. I promise."

"Almi, please. Let me just be there for you."

I smiled. "There's no winning with you, huh?"

"Not really." He chuckled.

"Like you said, I see us as friends as well. I will agree to talk to you whenever I feel overwhelmed about things. Fair enough?"

"I'll take that for now," he said, getting up to leave my office. "You sure you don't need me to hang around a little longer?"

"No, I'll be fine," I told him.

He walked around my desk and pulled me into a hug. I inhaled his Creed Aventus cologne. I recognized the scent because my brother used to wear it. It felt so good to be wrapped in his arms right now, and I took advantage of the moment by lying my head on his shoulder. When he gave me the infamous forehead kiss, my knees buckled, and I damn near slid to the floor.

"You sure you're good?" he asked, noticing I almost lost balance.

I laughed. "Yes, I'm good. Now go." I pulled away from our hug and shooed him away. "I'll see you in a couple of hours at the luncheon." He gave me a tender gaze and flashed a smile before he opened the door to head out. Lo and behold, Winnie's nosy ass was standing by my door ear hustling. I shook my head. This lady was just not going to give up at all. I don't know how long she had been standing there, but I can say there was nothing I did to give her anything to run back and say. I was honestly at the point I didn't give a shit for real though. I was going to head home after work and start working on my relationship with Kane before she could figure out something to do to ruin what we had left of it.

Chapter 10 Kane

If I would have known that sleeping with Zavia was going to cause such a big issue, I promise I wouldn't have. I was serious when I said it was going to be a one-time thing, but she wasn't having that. It had been two weeks now, and she was determined to keep things going, but I wanted to work on things with Almi. A few days ago when she came home from work, she demanded that we talk and put all of our thoughts and feelings on the table. I was glad we did, because we got a lot of issues squared away, and it was a moment of healing for us. I was no dummy though. I wasn't going to voluntarily tell her about my infidelity in no way, shape, or form.

I did tell her she made me feel like less than a man when I wasn't working and that she had become more distant since her mother had fallen ill. She told me I was pushing her away too during times she tried to be close and when she needed my support. She admitted she wasn't the easiest to deal with while I was unemployed, but she was frustrated with handling everything alone while it looked like all I did was play the video game. We both agreed that

I had started going out again too much lately, and we needed to put more effort into working on our relationship. We made mad love after our talk, and for the past few days, things have been going well.

Now back to Zavia. Old girl was straight bugging. She called and texted my phone endlessly. I did my best to dodge her at work, but she did everything she could to make her presence known. Who would have known that my putting it down on her the way I did would have her acting all crazy? So much for respecting Almi and knowing her place, because that went right out the window the night we decided to cross that line. I was getting to the point that I was about ready to block her damn number. To be on the safe side, I've been powering my phone off the second Almi walked through the door or when I walked through the door, depending on who was home first. I figured if any dire emergency came up with my mother or anything, she'd call Almi's phone when she saw she couldn't get through on mine. Almi saw this as an effort on my behalf to give her the time and attention she was craving, when in reality, I just wanted to save my ass.

I had just finished grading some tests and was about to leave my office to head home. I was doing good avoiding Zavia all day, up until now. Her ass popped up at my door, right as I was about to turn the lights off. She didn't look happy at all, and I knew she was in the mood for an argument, but I wasn't. She went from acting like my friend to acting like my woman, and it was time for me to set her ass straight.

"So that's how we're playing things now?" she blurted out, placing her hand on her hip.

"This is not the time or place for this right now, Zavia. Please don't bring that drama to our workplace." I scolded her.

"You got a whole lot of fucking nerve, Kane!" she yelled. "I give you the pussy, and then you do a one-eighty turn on my ass. I don't know who you think you I am, but you got the right one, and I got time today."

I snatched her into my office, and looked around to make sure no one was listening, before I closed the door. "Why the fuck would you make a scene at work, you silly ass woman?" I threw my hands up in frustration.

"How else am I supposed to get your attention when you won't answer my phone calls or reply to my text messages?"

I looked at her in disgust. She was no longer the attractive woman I once admired her to be. She was acting like a raging maniac, and at this point, I only saw her as the piece of ass she was. I really did value our friendship at first, but she knew what it was the night we had sex. I had made it plain from day one I had a woman and wasn't planning on leaving her. In my moment of weakness, I just wanted to relieve that built-up pressure from the nut that needed to be released, and I figured she wanted to do the same thing. I didn't start playing her ass until she kept coming at me about hooking up again. I kindly rejected her the first couple of times, but she wanted to keep pressing the issue, so I had to go another route, which was ignoring her ass.

"Why are you acting so childish all of a sudden? When I first met you, I thought you were on your grown woman shit." I shook my head.

"Oh, I'm a full-fledged, grown woman. However,

what I cannot deal with is a little boy who wanted to take advantage of this grown woman and thought he was gonna get that shit off."

"How the hell did I take advantage of you?"

"You talked all this mess about wanting to be faithful to your woman, and I respected that about you. Yet you knew what you were doing when you came crying to me about how bad things were going with y'all. You wanted to use that as a way to have sex with me."

"Zavia, listen to yourself. You sound silly as hell. We both were drinking and obviously horny in the moment, so that's why it happened. It shouldn't have happened, but it did. It was never my intention to play you. In fact, I wanted us to still be friends. I'm just not comfortable crossing that line with you again. I wanna work on things with my woman."

"So now you wanna work on things? You should have been working on things while you were busy working me."

"I can't do this," I said, opening my door to let her out of my office.

"You can, and you will. What makes you think you can just have sex with me then kick me to the curb like I'm some trash?"

"Zavia, leave my office now. Do not contact me anymore, and when we see each other here at work, don't even bother to look my way and speak."

"You are sadly mistaken if you think things will be that easy. Like I said, you messed with the wrong one. You will regret using me, Kane. Mark my words," she said, before rolling her eyes and walking down the hall.

I shook my head and locked my office door up. Zavia had completely lost it. I didn't have time to entertain this woman. She'd get the hint sooner or later. I went ahead and blocked her number as I made my way to my car. This lady was real-life crazy if she thought she was calling the shots. I don't know what type of weed she had been smoking, but that shit was killing her brain cells. I chuckled to myself as I got in my car and drove off.

I knew that neither of us were going to want to cook after a long day, so I stopped at Church's Chicken to get Almi and I one of those $5 boxes. Their chicken was greasy as hell, but it was so damn good, and after the stressful day I had, I could definitely go for some comfort food. I called Almi to tell her I had picked dinner up for us. She informed me that she had just arrived at the nursing home with her mother and would leave there in an hour to come straight home. I told her to take her time and would put our food in the oven on warm so I could keep the food hot, and we could eat together.

When I got home, I did as I said I would and headed to the bathroom to take a shower. When I stepped out, my phone was vibrating on the bathroom stand. I picked it up and saw I had four voicemail notifications. *Who the hell had called me that many times and that fast?* I didn't have any missed calls, which I thought was weird. I went to the visual voicemail option and saw that all the messages were coming from Zavia. I almost hurled my phone across the bathroom but thought twice because that would have been foolish to break my phone. I forgot I could block her number to keep her calls and texts from getting through, but that didn't stop her from being able to leave me a message. I deleted them, without even bothering to listen to them.

A noise from somewhere in the house startled me, and my heart began racing. My thumper was in the bedroom, so for now, I didn't have anything to defend myself with. I tried to calm down because it was probably just Almi. Maybe she decided to go ahead and come home sooner. I grabbed a towel and wrapped it around my waist before stepping out of the bathroom.

"Bae?" I called out. When I didn't get a response, I got nervous again. *Damn, did I even remember to lock the door behind me?* "Bae?"

I tiptoed through the house, nervous as hell. I don't care what nobody said. It didn't matter how macho you were, sometimes fear could consume you too. I didn't like being caught off guard. I wasn't a fighter for real, so my only choice was to make it to my bedroom to get my gun. I didn't hear anything else and thought that maybe I had only imagined hearing a noise earlier. I laughed at myself for being silly and acting so scary and flipped the light on when I got to my room. I about passed the fuck out at what I saw before me.

Zavia was lying butt ass naked across my bed with her head propped up on her hand. She smiled, rolled on her back, and started playing with her pussy. I ain't gonna lie, that shit had me aroused, and I know my dick stood at attention. For a second, I almost forgot how mad I was at her and was about to dive in for the bait. I caught myself though and snapped back to reality when I realized that not only was there a woman naked in me and Almi's bed, but I wondered how the hell she got into my house.

"What the fuck is wrong with you? Get up, and get out!" I yelled, snatching her up on the bed.

"I told you I won't be ignored," she said in a sing-song voice like the shit was funny. "Where is your precious Almi? Go ahead and fuck me right quick before she gets home, and I'll be on my way."

"You are really sick. How the hell did you get in my house?"

"You two don't do a good job of hiding your spare key," she said, pointing to the key she had placed on the nightstand. I guess she was right because under the flowerpot was just too damn typical.

"Get the fuck outta my house right now before I call the police on you for breaking and entering!"

"OK, OK," she said, getting up from the bed and throwing her hands up in defense.

"Don't you ever pull any shit like this again, or I will shoot your ass," I told her, grabbing my gun out the nightstand drawer.

"So you really wanna take it there, huh?" she said, smirking at me. She really didn't have it all. Either she wasn't scared, or she didn't believe I would shoot her.

I grabbed her arm roughly, picked up her clothes, and pushed her down the hall and out the door. On my cell phone, I dialed the 9 and the 1 and showed it to her so she'd see I wasn't playing. She took the hint and walked across the street to her car. I shook my head and slammed my door. I was in total disbelief of everything that was happening. I quickly got dressed, snatched the covers off the bed, put them in the washer, and put a new cover across the bed. I got some rose petals out the closet that I had left over from me and Almi's last romantic night and spread them across the bed and floor. I didn't want Almi becoming suspicious and asking any questions about the cover being changed. Maybe when she saw the rose petals, she would assume I changed the covers to make everything fresh and romantic for her. Maybe I was overthinking things, and it was just my guilt taking over.

I was so consumed in covering my tracks that I didn't notice Almi had come in the door. I jumped out my skin when she spoke and a smile came across her face when she saw what I had done.

"You are so sweet," she said.

"Y-Y-You scared me," was all I could manage to say.

She gave me a weird look and shrugged. "What's the occasion?"

"It's just that I love you, baby. You actually got here a little sooner than I thought. I wanted to run you a bath and light candles for you too," I told her.

"Well, don't let that stop you. You can still do your thang," she said. "I'm starving. Where's the food?"

I watched as she kicked her heels off and started making her way toward the kitchen. "It's in the oven!" I yelled after her. "Here I come."

I gave everything a once-over and made sure Zavia didn't leave any piece of clothing behind. When I was satisfied that everything was in order, I joined Almi in the kitchen, who had already taken our food out the oven and was putting it on plates for us.

"I see we're out of wine. I'm going to have to make a quick run to the store," she said.

"We don't need any wine tonight, baby," I said, still feeling nervous.

"Yes, we do. Dierberg's is only five minutes away. You can run my bath while I run to the store. When I get back, it'll be on and popping," she said.

"I guess that'll work," I told her. Maybe I could use the few moments alone to get myself together and clear my head. Right now, I was on edge, and I was sure Almi could tell because I wasn't doing a good job of masking it. We made small talk while we ate dinner, and I couldn't wait for her to finish so she could go. It's crazy how the entire situation messed up my mood that fast, but I promised myself I would be straight once I got the chance to regroup.

My dad called as Almi put away the dishes. I was going to let the call roll over to voicemail, but I went ahead and took it. "Hello?"

"Hey, son. You got a minute?" he asked.

"What's up, Dad? Yeah, I do," I said.

Almi looked at me when she heard me respond to him and rolled her eyes. I could tell she didn't care too much for him, and she said it was because she felt he had some type of ulterior motive for popping into my life out of nowhere. I told her to let me worry about that, and she didn't say anything else about it. Although she kept quiet, that didn't stop her from showing her dislike of him whenever she got the chance.

Do you want anything from the store? she mouthed.

I shook my head no and turned my attention back to the phone.

"I need to talk to you about something, son," he said.

"I'll be back," Almi whispered. I nodded as she headed out the door.

"What's going on?" I asked him.

"Son, I'm sick, and I need a favor from you," he said.

"You're sick. What's wrong?"

"Kane, I'm in need of a kidney. Would you mind coming to my next doctor's appointment with me to see if you're a match and donating it to me?" he asked, completely catching me off guard.

"Wow, Dad. That's a lot to ask somebody. Um… that's something I need to think about," I told him.

"Hmm… That definitely was not the answer I was expecting, but I understand."

"I mean… look, this is something we need to discuss in person and not over the phone."

My line beeped, and when I looked to see who it was, I saw it was Winnie. I wondered if he had asked her. Something told me he did, but she wasn't a match, so he was coming to me. This was a big deal, and I wanted to help him if I could, but I needed to really weigh the pros and cons. What if I gave him a kidney and my other one failed later? I hoped that would never be the case, but you just didn't know.

"Hey, Winnie's beeping in on the other line. I'll call you back," I told him.

"That's fine. Just call me and let me know when you'd like to talk in person," he said.

I clicked over to answer Winnie's call without giving him a response. "What's up, sis?" I answered.

"Hey, bro. How are you?" she asked.

"I'm good, and you?" I replied.

"I'm good. You got a minute?" she inquired.

What the hell was going on today that everybody needed a minute of my time? I was already feeling overwhelmed and still needed a few moments to myself before Almi got back. "To what do I owe the pleasure of your call?" I asked her.

"I need to holler at you about your girl Almi," she said.

Chapter 11 Almi

I came to the store for one thing and somehow ended up with a cart full of extra stuff. I needed to hurry up and get my butt out of this store and back home to Kane. I was so grateful that things had started getting better between us. For a minute, it was like I didn't know who he was any more, but we finally got things back on track. Lord knows I missed how good he made love to me, and he has been showing out these past few days. He always did his thing and left me sore between the legs, and that only meant he was hitting it right. I had a couple of days to recoup, so I was ready to get exclusive with my man tonight.

I had just about wrapped things up in the store and was ready to get in line, but this eerie feeling came over me. It felt like I was being watched, and I had always learned to follow my gut instinct. I looked around me, and nothing seemed out of the ordinary. I shrugged it off and proceeded toward checkout. I couldn't shake the feeling though, and when I turned around, all I saw was some woman walking behind me. Nothing seemed too out of the ordinary about her, except she didn't have a shopping cart, basket, or anything in her hand. I noticed her in a couple of aisles with me previously, but again, that wasn't too strange.

I went to self-checkout, and she seemed to just linger there. I kept glancing over at her, and she appeared to be watching me too. Nothing about her looked familiar, but I had to admit that she was very pretty. Maybe I was overthinking things, and she wasn't tripping off of me after all. I finished ringing out my groceries, bagged them, and headed to my car. However, when I noticed her leave the store right behind me, damn near on my heels, I was about ready to curse her ass out.

"Um, may I help you?" I turned around so fast, damn near snapping my neck in the process.

"Yes you may," she replied with so much attitude that she caught me off guard. I could definitely say I wasn't expecting that shit at all.

I realized was blocking the entrance when a couple of people had to say excuse me to get by, so I moved to the side with my cart so this woman could state her case and go on about her business. "OK, who are you?" I asked, trying to match her attitude.

"My name is Zavia, and I work with Kane," she said matter-of-factly.

"What does that have to do with me?" I asked her, really wondering what the hell she wanted at this point.

"I just thought you should know the type of man you have. He's quite, umm… how can I put this?" she said, looking up at the sky and tapping her lip with her finger like she was really thinking. "He's been unfaithful to you."

"Why do you feel the need to be the one to tell me this?" I asked her, not wanting her to know what she said was getting to me. She had confirmed my worst fears about why Kane had been acting strange. I had heard so many stories about the side chick confronting the wife or girlfriend, but I never thought it would happen to me. At the end of the day, I had to stand my ground and not allow her to see that she had my feathers ruffled. Kane was about to get a whole lot of lip when I got back home though.

"I just thought you may want to know. Kane and I have been messing around for some time now. I had to call it quits when he became a little rough, if you know what I mean," she hinted.

"Well, you served your purpose by telling me. Have a good evening," I told her, beginning to push my cart out the store.

"Don't you want to see the pictures?" she called out after me.

I stopped dead in my tracks. She had pictures? In the back of my mind, I was hoping this was just some random ass chick wanting to start something and Kane would convince me that she was lying. She just said she had pictures though, so part of me felt compelled to see them.

"What pictures?" I asked, in barely above a whisper. I was losing the battle because my eyes were beginning to fill with tears, afraid of what I was about to see.

She pulled out her phone and showed me pictures of them hanging out at a bar. She took it a step further and showed me video of them drinking and making out at her place. I wondered if Kane even knew she was recording this stuff. They were kissing and undressing each other in her living room before making their way off camera, likely to her bedroom. I couldn't stop the tears from flowing. What really fucked me all the way up was the last picture she showed me. This bitch was lying across my bed ass naked. It was one thing to be a dog and cheat, but it was a completely different ball game and the maximum disrespect to do that shit in our home.

Chapter 12 Almi

"Kane! Kaaaaane!" I yelled as I stormed through the front door like a mad man. This asshole had a whole lot of explaining to do. The reality was, no matter what he said, it would change or fix what he did. There was no lying to get out of this one. There was no turning back from this, and I already knew we were done.

"Yeah, baby?" he said, emerging from the bathroom. "I just finished running your bath water, so it's nice and hot for you."

"Fuck you, and fuck that bath water! How could you!" I said, punching him in his chest. He held his hands up to block any further blows from me.

"What are you talking about, baby?"

"Who is Zavia?" I asked him.

A shocked look came across his face like he was surprised that I knew who he was, but he quickly tried to cover up his look of surprise by acting all nonchalant. "Aw, Zavia, bae... she's just my co-worker. Why?" he asked.

"Why? Motherfucker, did you just ask me why!" I continued to yell. I was pissed off, and he knew I was on ten because I rarely cursed.

"Yeah. *Why?*" he asked, almost too defensively for me.

"Because the bitch was following me around the store and then came to me and told me y'all was fucking!" I screamed.

"She's delusional. A woman will tell you anything just so she can get what's yours, bae. I ain't fuck that girl. She's been trying to get with me forever, but I've been dodging her. I guess she's just mad."

I picked the candle holder up off the dining room table and hurled it at him. It hit him in his temple, and his hand quickly flew to that spot. He looked at me in shock that I had hit him, but then got angry, grabbed my shoulders, and shook me.

"Girl, what the hell is wrong with you? Don't you ever put your hands on me or throw anything at me like that again," he yelled.

"Fuck you!" I spit in his face.

He lifted his hand to hit me, but then caught himself. He picked up an empty champagne glass off the table and threw it against the wall instead and yelled out in frustration. "I could fucking kill you, girl! To spit on somebody is the most disgusting shit ever."

"You didn't have a problem swapping spit with that bitch! I bet you didn't know she recorded y'all at her place, huh? I already know you fucked her. Then you had the nerve to have that bitch in our house! In our bed!"

"I didn't have her in this house," he said, looking confused.

"So the picture she showed me lying ass naked in our bed was photoshopped, huh?" I said sarcastically. "I guess that's why you had to change the sheets, after you fucked her on them."

"OK, Almi. OK. Yes, I fucked up and had sex with that girl, but it was just one time at her place. I never had her in our house though baby. You gotta believe me."

"And why should I? Especially when I saw the picture."

A look of realization came over his face, and he blew out a breath. "Look, bae, just hear me out. Like I said, I fucked up. I told her we couldn't keep messing around, but she wouldn't let me call things off. She kept calling me and texting me, but I was ignoring her because I already told her I wanted to work on things with you. She must have followed me home, because when I was in the shower, she let herself in with the key you left under the flowerpot. I would never do no fucked-up shit like have sex in our home or in our bed?"

"Oh, you'll just do fucked-up shit like have sex with someone else period though?" I looked at him in disgust. I couldn't believe all of this was unfolding right now. The love of my life had broken something sacred between us. I was so sure he would ask me to marry him one day, but now, that would never happen. I couldn't believe the turn my life had just taken.

"Almi. Baby. I know saying that I'm sorry won't fix this situation, but I am. I promise it will never happen again," he began to beg.

"I know it won't happen again, because I'm not going to let it," I said, storming to our bedroom.

I snatched my luggage from the back of our closet and began packing it with my things. I was going to go stay at my parents' house. I was glad I didn't sell it like I initially wanted to. The yearly property taxes on it weren't going to be too much, and the house only needed minor repairs. I figured I might as well keep it, fix it up, and whenever Kane and I had a family, I was hoping to move into it. None of what I imagined was ever going to happen now.

Kane continued trying to reason to with me and did everything he could to get me to stay. He pulled at my arm a couple of times, and I gave him a look to let him know not to mess with me. He about lost his mind a few minutes ago when he grabbed at my shoulders. I knew I shouldn't have spit on him, because he was right, that was gross as hell. I was mad though and not thinking clearly. As soon as I finished packing my bags, I made my way to the car.

The crazy thing is that I've cried so much that no more tears would fall now. This is a time I thought I would have been hysterical, and I was at first, but now I was more angry than anything. I didn't even know Kane any more. The man I thought I knew would have never done anything like this to hurt me. Here it is, the bitch gave me all the proof I needed, and he still wanted to deny sleeping with her in our home. As soon as I got to my parents' house, I was taking a shower and scrubbing the hell out of my skin. He done had sex with this woman in our bed, and I laid in those very sheets and cum stains. I almost threw up in my mouth thinking about it.

\ I pulled up to my mother's house and fumbled with my key and luggage as I got out of the car. I let myself in and damn near jumped out of my skin when I saw someone sitting in the dark on the couch.

"It's me, Almi," my brother Alan said before I could scream or run back out the door.

I quickly flipped on a light switch. "What are you doing here, Alan, and why are you sitting in the dark?"

"This is *our* mother's house. I'm not welcome here or something?"

"I mean, you haven't been coming by or trying to be involved in anything. Why are you here now?"

"My girlfriend kicked me out about a week ago, so I've been staying here," he replied.

"In the dark?" I asked sarcastically.

"No, I was sitting in the dark and thinking right now."

"I guess." I sighed, plopping down in a chair across from him.

"What are *you* doing here while you're questioning me?"

"Because like you said, it's our mother's house. Well, our parents' house. However, if you must know, Kane and I broke up."

"I'm sorry to hear that," he said.

"Likewise. It looks like we both run home when the going gets tough, huh?"

"It appears that way."

"What happened with you and... what's her name?" I asked him. I really didn't know his girlfriend's name because I never cared to. I met her once a few years ago, and she rubbed me wrong with the know-it-all attitude she had since she was an older woman.

"Tamara," he replied flatly.

"Yeah, her. So what happened with you two?" I asked him.

"I got sick of her treating me like a child. I get that she's ten years my senior, but at the end of the day, I'm a man."

"How was she treating you like a child?"

"Demanding me to take the trash out, clean up, cook, and do other things as if I wasn't already helping. I promise I did those things, sis. I may not have done them when she wanted me to, but I did. She never considered the fact that I worked two jobs to help our household stay afloat just so she could work part-time and focus on her dream of achieving her master's degree."

For a minute, it was like déjà vu because it made me think of how I used to boss Kane around and demand him to do those things. He said I made him feel like less than a man when I did that. At first, I didn't want to hear it, but I figured he had a point. Listening to my brother say it only confirmed that what Kane said must be true. I knew men had their egos, and they wanted their women to respect their position as men. At the same time, our men needed to understand we did need help. It's possible that we sometimes took advantage of having the upper hand, like by Tamara being older than Alan, and me being the one who worked while Kane didn't. It wasn't to be out of order though. Sometimes we just needed to know that *we* weren't being taken advantage of. I've watched enough movies, read plenty of books, and listened to other women tell stories about their no-good men. Thinking about those things made a person think smart and want to be ahead of the game to keep from falling victim to bad circumstances.

"You two have been together for so long. You don't think you can just talk to her and work things out?" I suggested.

"I tried talking, and I'm done talking. I slipped up and asked her why she's being such a bitch about things. That's when she slapped me and put me out." He shrugged.

"You called her a bitch!" I exclaimed.

"See? Y'all hear what the hell y'all want to hear. I did not *call* her a bitch. I asked why is she *acting* like a bitch about things."

"Same damn difference, Alan. You can't use the word bitch in any way, shape, or form when referring to women. It's just plain disrespectful."

"Whatever, Almi. I'm really not in the mood for this conversation." He sighed.

I threw my hands up in defense. "OK, I'll back off. Sorry for asking. Well, if you care to know—" I started to say.

"I don't," he replied.

"Alan, shut up and listen!" I chuckled, throwing a pillow at him.

"Well, even though you don't care to know, I'm telling anyway. Kane and I broke up because I found out he was cheating."

"How did you find out?" he asked, looking serious at this point. He was in full big brother mode now.

"The woman he was messing around with actually approached me in the grocery store and showed me pictures and a video of them booed up. She even showed me a picture of them having sex in our bed."

"In your bed!" he jumped up angrily. "Dude done took that shit way too far now, sis. Where is he at? The crib?"

"Calm down, Alan," I said, placing my hand on his

arm. "There was a picture of her lying across the bed naked. Kane swore up and down he did not have sex with her in the bed, but she used the spare key to let herself in, and when he got out the shower, she was there."

"I told you a long time ago, under the flowerpot was a stupid ass place to put an extra key. That shit is way too obvious."

"Yeah, Kane warned me about that a long time ago."

"Do you believe him?"

"About what, sleeping with her? I know for a fact he slept with her because he admitted to that."

"The story about her using the spare key to let herself in and him not sleeping with her in your bed?"

"I don't know. It's possible, but the fact that he even crossed that line and cheated in the first place makes me skeptical to believe anything else he has to say. Should I believe him?"

"Hell, sis, I don't know. That's your damn relationship. You need some female friends to talk to about this shit."

"Really, Alan! Just a second ago you were about to go kung fu Joe on his ass." I chuckled. "Now you don't want to talk about it?"

"You're my little sister, and I don't like seeing you hurt or upset. Any big brother would react that way. I just can't give you advice or my opinion because I'm a man, so I don't know."

"Oh my God! Don't tell me you cheated on Tamara before." I rolled my eyes.

"Yeah, a couple of years ago," he replied nonchalantly.

"Why, bro? Why would you do that!"

"It was a one-time thing. I was hanging out with my boys, got drunk, and made a dumb decision with a chick I met at the club that night. It was a one-night stand."

"Does she know?"

"Yes, we talked about it, and obviously she forgave me, and we worked past it."

"I'm not sure if I can forgive Kane. This was a hard blow, and it hurt my heart to the core. It was one of his co-workers, so this is someone he'll have to continue to see."

"Again, sis, you have to make the final decision on whether you want to work through things or not. It took Tamara a couple of weeks to talk to me when I cheated, but we finally figured things out. I was wrong, and I feel like she deserved better than that. I'm sure Kane loves you. Y'all been together this long. I still don't like the fact that he hurt you, but we all have our moments of weakness."

I heard what he was saying, but right now, everything was too fresh for me to try to think logically. If he was weak once, he could become weak again. I couldn't fathom betraying Kane in any type of way. I *almost* kissed Marshall, but I didn't. Kane should have practiced better self-control. I just needed to sleep on it tonight, and I would decide what to do from here. I was pretty certain that I was finished with him, but only time would tell. Meanwhile, I needed to talk to Alan about our mother and his absence, hopefully, without offending him.

"What's been going on with you otherwise?" I asked him. "Where have you been when it comes to Mama?"

"Almi, I can't talk about that right now." He tried

to brush me off.

"If not now, then when, Alan? Mama's health is getting worse and worse, and you haven't been around to see her or help with her in any type of way."

"I did my part by making sure her funds were spent wisely, and she kept this house with all the bills paid," he said. He sounded like such a cold-hearted jerk right now. *How the hell could someone be like that about their mother?*

"That's a wonderful thing, and it's very much appreciated that you looked out for us in that way. Don't you think Mama would like to see you though? Aren't you the least bit concerned about her and how she's doing?

"Damn, Almi! Why do you have to keep pushing it!" He jumped up and began to pace the floor. I continued to watch him and noticed he was crying. I had hit a nerve, and it was about time he opened up to talk about it.

I got up and walked up to him, pulling him into a hug. I wanted him to know I was there for him, and we could get through this together. "Alan, talk to me. What's on your mind?"

"One minute, our mother was OK, and the next minute, her life was ripped from her, all because some asshole ran a red light. It's been hard for me to watch our mother become so dependent on us like she was our child. That shit hurt, Almi," he cried. He had finally confirmed my suspicion of why he pulled away from us like he did.

"It's been really hard on me too, but I've been doing what I have to do."

"It's such a heavy burden to bear. Then you were damn near grown, about to graduate high school in a couple of years and go off to college. This world is so fucked up, Almi, and I knew I couldn't hold you back and protect you. I didn't want you to go away and something happen to you too. Low key, I was happy you decided to stay local for college. Then our father was killed while serving this fucked-up ass country we live in. I was forced to be the man of the house at nineteen! That was so unfair! I didn't even get a chance to experience the world because I had to hang around to make sure you and Mama were OK. I had other dreams to fulfill, but I couldn't. No, I wasn't front and center like I should have been and more involved like you wanted me to be, but I couldn't stand the idea of looking my reality right in the face. It was too hard for me to do."

I never understood my brother felt that way, and I was glad he was finally talking and opening up. Life wasn't easy, and he felt his chance to experience life was ripped from him. He was attending our local community college for the paralegal program when our mother was involved in that car accident. He had the hopes of transferring to another college to get his bachelor's degree and going off to law school one day. He wanted to leave St. Louis and experience the world, but he didn't. One of the reasons I attended college locally was to be near our mother. I stayed on campus so I could experience the social life, but I spent every weekend at home. My mother had a support worker and home health-care worker to make sure she was fine during the week. She was still able to do some things on her own once her injuries had healed. It wasn't until the past few months that her health began to decline.

"Alan, I get it. I promise I do, and I won't hold that against you. I just wish you would go see Mama. Things seem like they're taking a turn for the worse, and it would be good if you could see her before… you know…" My voice trailed off.

"Mama's d-dying?" He seemed alarmed.

"Not right now, but being honest with you, I'm sure it's coming. The doctors are constantly running tests. It seems the Alzheimer's is moving through the stages a little too quickly. I can feel it. Something ain't right, and they need to figure out what it is."

"When are you going to go see her again?" he asked.

"I'm up there every day. I'll go after work tomorrow. You coming?"

"What time?"

"After five p.m."

"I get off at six. I'll come then."

"Good. I'll stay up there and wait if you want me to. I usually leave as soon as she eats dinner."

"Please stay. I may need your support."

I promised him I would. I gave him some alone time while I went upstairs to my old room. I needed some time alone as well to sort through my thoughts. I was glad Alan and I finally made peace with this situation about my mother. We still had a long road ahead. Meanwhile, the unexpected with Kane was a detour in my own personal path in life. I started to wonder if cheating in return would make me feel better.

Chapter 13 Kane

I don't know how the hell all of this back fired on me so fast. Everything went south before I even had the chance to blink. Winnie had told me about Almi and some guy at their office named Marshall she believed Almi may be messing around with. I thought my sister might have just been tripping, so I was going to ask Almi about it to get an understanding and move past it. Unfortunately, that didn't happen because that crazy bitch Zavia had gotten to her and told her everything. She even went so far as to take pictures of herself in our bed, and that made things even worse than they actually were.

I still couldn't believe her crazy ass had let herself into our house. I had no idea this lady had some type of *Fatal Attraction* type of thing to her. She did well playing that little role like she didn't want to come between us. I blamed myself for opening that door in the first place because she had stayed in her place on up until then. I had so many regrets right now, but since I couldn't go back to fix it, all I could do was go forward and do my best to convince Almi that I loved her and needed her. I didn't want Zavia or any other woman. I promise I had learned my lesson after this one. I wouldn't do anything to ever hurt her again if she could just forgive me for this moment of weakness.

Three days had gone by, and Almi still hadn't called or come home. She was ignoring my phone calls and text messages. I was having flowers and a card sent to her job today because I was too afraid to go and get embarrassed by her. I was almost certain she was staying at her parents' home if she wasn't at a hotel. A part of me really did want to go to her job to see about this Marshall guy, because I was afraid that if what Winnie told me wasn't true, it might become true. I knew that when women were vulnerable like this, it was much easier for another man to swoop in and shoot his shot.

I sat at my desk at work catching up on entering grades in the system. The weird thing was that I had not seen Zavia since I put her out my house. She must have been calling in to work, or she was doing a really good job of staying out of my way. She was probably embarrassed, and rightfully so, because she made a complete ass of herself. All she had to do was a take a hint the first time around, and it wouldn't have come to his point. If someone is telling you he or she doesn't want you, then take heed and leave that person alone. All of this transpired for nothing.

Meanwhile, I needed to get back to my father about what he asked me. I was so caught up in trying to get Almi to talk to me that I had forgotten about him and what he asked me that day. I thought it was a pretty bold move, especially since we just met each other. I was now starting to wonder if that was the reason he came back into my life in the first place. I thought he really wanted to get to know me as his son, when he knew he was sick and found me just so he could ask for my kidney. I didn't want to believe that and wanted to convince myself that it was just my mind wandering, but deep down, I knew there had to be some truth to what I was thinking.

I was almost finished entering grades into the system when a knock came at my office door. I called out to whoever it was to come in, and got the shock of my life when I saw my supervisor and two police officers. My heart started racing, and I was praying that nothing had happened to Almi. I was afraid to hear what this visit was pertaining to because Lord knows I couldn't tolerate any bad news right now.

"Mr. Williamson, these officers would like to speak with you about a very important matter. I need you to come with us to my office please," my supervisor, Carl, said.

I slowly got up from my desk, wondering what this was all about. Why couldn't he just break the bad news to me right then and there? It didn't make any sense to prolong things by making me take what looked like some the walk of shame. My co-workers were glancing up from their desks as we walked by or passed them in the hallway with these knowing looks. I caught a couple of them raising their eyebrows, and another instructor who I was usually cool with rolled her eyes and shook her head. The closer we got to Carl's office, something told me this was about way more than I assumed. A little relief started to set in when I realized it must not be about Almi; however, nervousness began to consume me as my suspicion

171

increased.

"Please, take as seat, Mr. Willamson," Carl said.

We were normally on a first-name basis, so I thought it was strange he was being so formal right now. One of the officers sat in the chair next to mine, and the other stood guard at the door once he closed it. Carl cleared his throat and gave me a very stern look.

"It has been brought to my attention that an unfortunate event has taken place." Carl began. I felt sick to my stomach. *Lord, please tell me nothing happened to Almi after all.* He cleared his throat before he continued speaking. "Our officers are here to ask you a few questions about this incident."

"Hello, I'm Officer Gandy, and this is my partner, Officer Sparks," he said, gesturing to the one standing guard. "Our detective is away in a conference for the day, so he sent us out to speak with you. He will likely be in touch with you to follow-up after this."

"W-What's going on?" I stuttered.

"It's apparent that you know Zavia Brown because you work with her. How well do you know her outside of the workplace?'

"I know Zavia pretty well… on a friendship level," I said, confused about why they were asking me about her.

"She has filed a formal complaint saying you raped her," Officer Gandy said.

"There is no way that I raped that woman!" I yelled out.

"That is for us to complete an investigation and decide. We would like you to come down to the station with us to answer a few more questions," Officer Gandy stated.

"Am I under arrest?" I asked.

"Not at this time. I can assure you once the detective returns tomorrow, he'll put in that you're wanted for questioning. You can go ahead and come down to the station and get this questioning over with, or we can return to your job or home to pick you up tomorrow." He tried to reason with me.

"If I may," Carl interjected, nodding to Officer Gandy. "Mr. Williamson, I think it's best you go ahead and go with them. This type of um… *exposure*, for lack of better words, in the workplace is not good for you or the school. Please just go ahead and get this over with. Meanwhile, I am placing both you and Ms. Brown on leave until we know what is going on with you two."

"Are you serious?" I asked, jumping up.

"Whoa there. Calm down," Officer Sparks said from where he was standing.

I couldn't believe the turn my life had begun to take in just seventy-two hours. I wasn't under arrest, so I didn't have to go, but as they said, they'd come again for me anyway. I needed to get an attorney because I was being accused of a very serious crime that I damn sure didn't commit. Didn't this crazy broad just break into my house the other day, and here she is filing charges against me? False charges at that. What part of the game was this because I damn sure was losing it? So many thoughts were running through my head right now. I didn't even know where the hell to begin. I didn't have any money for a lawyer. We used all of our savings when I was out of work, and I hadn't had a chance to start saving money again. I knew Almi always kept money put up for a rainy day, but there was no way she would help me with this one, especially since I had hurt her. I didn't know what to do right now.

"Mr. Williamson?" Carl said, bringing me back to my cruel reality. "Your choice on whether or not you'll go ahead with these officers, but I do need you to exit the building at this time."

I looked at him with disgust and just shook my head. There was no way I was going with these officers and leaving my car here. I figured it wouldn't hurt to follow them down to the station because I was completely innocent anyway. Maybe we could get all of this squared away today, and I could go on about my business. I couldn't afford to be out on leave, so I might as well handle this now so Carl could see that all of this was a big misunderstanding.

My stomach felt like it was in knots as I followed the police to the station. A couple of times I almost decided to make a different turn and go on about my business, but I figured that would only make me look guilty and help them build a case. I knew it was foolish of me to speak to them without a lawyer, but since I didn't have the money for one, I didn't have a choice. I wanted to be confident that my innocence would be good enough, but I knew there were way too many people in prison for crimes they didn't commit. Missouri's justice system was fucked up, and I prayed like hell I didn't say or do anything to make myself look bad or guilty.

When we pulled in, they showed me where I could park my car. I hesitated to get out but blew out a breath and stepped out my car slowly. I drug my feet behind them, and I could tell I was aggravating them by moving so slowly, but for some reason I had a bad feeling about all of this. Hell, I was still looking for the camera crew to jump out and say this was a prank. Unfortunately, this was real life and currently *my* life. Each step I took, my feet felt heavier, and I was experiencing so many emotions. I was nauseated, felt like I was going to pee on myself, and my heart was beating so hard I thought I was going to pass out. I was actually relieved to take a seat in the room they placed me in because I felt like my knees were going to buckle from all the pressure.

"Thank you for making this easy and coming down to the station with us," Officer Gandy said.

"I really don't understand what's going on. I didn't rape that girl. We only had sex one time, and it was mutual," I told them.

"Allow us to ask the questions here," Officer Sparks said. I glared at him and felt my lip twitch. I already knew how this shit went from watching enough TV shows. There was always a good cop and a bad cop, just so the good cop could pretend to be your friend, get you to trust him, and confess. In this case, I didn't have anything to confess.

"Ms. Brown said that three nights ago, you invited her back to your place, and you got a little rough with her. She continued to turn you down, but you forced yourself onto her and raped her," Officer Gandy stated.

"That's not true, officer. She used a key to let herself into my home, and when I stepped out the shower, she was in my bed. I put her out my home before my girlfriend could arrive and catch her there."

"She stated you put her out after you raped her,"

Officer Sparks said.

"Why the hell would I invite someone where I lay my head to rape them, knowing the shit would come back on me?" I yelled.

"I don't know, you tell me," Officer Sparks replied sarcastically.

"Look, I told you what happened. This interrogation makes absolutely no sense right now," I said.

"Then explain these," Officer Sparks said, pulling out the photos.

"What the fuck?" I whispered, when I saw them. This girl done lost every fiber of her being. She done did some straight *Thin Line Between Love and Hate* type of shit and caused some bruises to herself. She took photos of bruises on her chest, shoulders, arms, and legs. As I was looking at the photos, Officer Gandy pulled out his phone to show me a couple of videos. There was one of her sitting her car crying in her panties and bra from the night I put her out. She said how I had raped her and she had to break free from me, that's why she didn't have time to put her clothes on. This crazy ass girl thought up an elaborate scheme to get me back for not fucking her again. Who the fuck raised this girl?

"Officers, I promise this is a huge misunderstanding. Can you all please just allow me to tell my side of the story?" I begged, needing for them to understand this chick was fraudulent.

"We're listening," Officer Gandy said gently. Again, I already knew he was playing the good guy role and would get me to do anything to admit fault when I wasn't wrong.

I cleared my throat and told them everything from how I met Zavia, how she promised to stay in her lane and respect my relationship, how I fucked up and crossed that line, and how she started stalking me. When I was finished, Officer Gandy nodded, and Officer Sparks shook his head. Neither one of them looked like they believe me.

"If this were the case, Mr. Williamson, why didn't you file a report for harassment, stalking, or even her breaking into your house?" Officer Sparks asked.

"I'm a whole man. What I look like filing a report for some mess like that?"

"Because you're lying. Why *wouldn't* you file one?"

I rubbed my temples and yelled out in frustration. What didn't these two understand about what I was saying? Why are they making this so difficult? I was the victim here, and instead, she had these folks feeling sorry for her. I had to admit that things did look bad because she had all these damn bruises from God knows where and then I failed to make a report about her. These officers knew that would get my man card revoked if I reported some shit like that. Now I wish I would have. They exchanged glances, and Officer Sparks nodded his head toward the door for Officer Grady to follow him. They left me there alone for about ten minutes before they came back and gave me the third degree again.

They were so determined to get me to admit to something I didn't do. Now I see why people made confessions about crimes they didn't commit because this shit here was mentally exhausting and driving me crazy. I was to the point that I was about to give in because I was tired of sitting here. They didn't have a thing on me, and I felt like deep down they knew that Zavia was clever as hell with the whole bruise thing.

When they saw they weren't getting anywhere with the questioning, they began reading me my rights and put me under arrest. I was in complete shock that I couldn't even argue with them. I never admitted to anything, and they still chose to charge me. I already knew they couldn't hold me for over twenty-four hours without having a warrant served. I was pretty sure they would convince the prosecutor to do just that with the false evidence they had against me. I don't know how the hell my day turned upside down like it did, but this shit here was crazy. I knew Almi didn't want to hear from me, but I didn't know who else to call.

Chapter 14 Almi

"You have a call at no expense from 'Kane', an inmate at St. Louis County Jail. Press five to accept the call. Press six to block calls to this number from this facility," the recording said when I answered my phone from a number I didn't recognize. My heart was racing. What the hell was Kane doing in jail, and why was he calling me of all people? He knew I was mad as hell at him, and his being in jail wouldn't change that.

I pushed five and listened to the recording tell me the call could be monitored and recorded. I hesitated to say hello, but he spoke up as soon as he realized the call was connected. "Hello!" he yelled into the phone. "Almi, you there?"

"What, Kane? Why are you calling me from jail?" I asked him, sounding a little more annoyed than I intended to, but hell, that's how I felt.

"Man, that crazy ass broad had me arrested. She filed a police report and said I raped her."

"Are you serious!" I exclaimed. "Why would she go and do some crazy mess like that?" I asked, totally shocked at what I was hearing. I was mad as hell at him, but I knew he wasn't the type to rape someone.

"Yes. I need a lawyer fast. I'm on leave at work because the police came to my job to get me, but I promise to pay you back as soon as I can," he said all in one breath.

"Hold on now, Kane! Who said I was going to give you money for a lawyer?" I stopped him.

"Really, Almi? I'm your man. Why wouldn't you help me?"

"My *man* wouldn't have done what he did by cheating on me and having another woman in our house. How the hell I know you *didn't* rape that girl. You have been acting real strange lately and sometimes I don't think I know who you are any more," I said.

"Come on now, baby. Don't do me like that," he begged.

"Kane, you're calling the wrong person. I can't help you," I said, hanging up on him.

I plopped down on my mother's sofa. It had been a long day at work and dinner with my mother was emotionally draining. I didn't know how much more I could take. Tears began to roll down my face. Kane called back twice, but each time, I let it roll to voicemail. Of course I didn't want Kane in jail, but I was still mad, so it served him right to sit his butt there for a couple of days. I hated saying what I said to him, because I just couldn't see him taking things *that* far with that woman. I couldn't see Kane cheating on me either though, and he did that. In my heart, I knew he didn't commit that crime, so I was sure he'd be fine in a couple of days. At least I hoped so anyway. I needed some time to think, and maybe if he called back tomorrow to update me on everything, I would consider helping him get an attorney. For now, I just wanted to take a shower and get some rest.

Alan had still been hanging out around here, so who knows how long it would be before him and his girl decided to make up. I have to admit, I liked having him around for the company, because our parents' house was just too damn big to be alone in. I smiled to myself as I quickly showered and lie down in my old bed. The tears continued to flow as I reminisced to my childhood. I had really good memories of my family and I, so it hurt like hell that it all ended way too soon. Sometimes I hated the direction my life had taken, but I knew these things only made me stronger in the end.

I fell asleep with so much on my mind that I tossed and turned. I was in and out of sleep, and each time, my dream was different. I dreamed about Kane going to prison and Zavia laughing because neither one of us had him. I dreamed about my daddy being alive and my mother being well. I even dreamed about Alan and his girlfriend getting married. I woke up feeling exhausted and about ready to call in so I could try getting some more rest. I had some important accounts I needed to update today, so I couldn't call in, and I guess coffee was just going to have to be my best friend.

I pulled into work this morning, looked in the mirror, and noticed bags under my eyes. I touched up my make up before I got out the car so I could look half decent today. I felt like crap, but I didn't need for my look to match it. I stepped out my car and held my head high like I always did, ready to tackle the work day. I headed straight for the break room to get my coffee and ran right into

Winnie and Marshall. They were chatting away, and I greeted both of them. Winnie mumbled a hello and Marshall smiled so big that it lit up the room.

"Oh, Winnie. Your brother is in county jail. You might want to call up there and see what's going on," I told her after I finished pouring my coffee. I didn't wait for her response and left right out the break room.

Marshall walked close behind me, asking me to wait up. I slowed down a little, so we could walk together. He took my coffee out my hand and held it for me while I opened the door to my office. I tousled my hair a little, already feeling overwhelmed by the work tasks I had before me. I had been doing good keeping my panic attacks under control. I thought I would have lost it when I found out about Kane and his mistress, but surprisingly, I held my composure. I didn't know how much longer I could stay in one piece though, so I looked in my purse for my pills and popped one.

"You good?" Marshall asked, raising a brow.

"I will be in a moment," I told him.

"What's this talk of your boyfriend being in jail?"

"It's a long story." I sighed.

"I have time," he said.

"No. Actually, you don't. You need to get to work and take care of those files on your desk. That information needs to be entered in by the end of the day, and you probably want to make sure those figures are correct," I instructed him.

"That'll get done. Don't worry about me. I am worried about you though. You've really been throwing yourself into your job these past couple days, barely taking breaks or coming out of your office for air. You've been cordial but not quite yourself. I wanted to give you time to process whatever is bothering you, but now it's time to talk," he said.

"Marshall, I really don't want to talk," I said quietly, typing away at my computer keys and purposely keeping my eyes glued to the monitor."

"You promised me you would though." He reminded me.

"I guess you have a point. Close my door," I told him.

I took a deep breath before I began. I told him everything that happened with Zavia on up to Kane calling me last night telling me he was arrested and why. I also told him I was still stressing over my mother, but it was also nice to have Alan's support now. He went with me the past couple of days to see her after work before he went off to a bar.

"That's a huge load for you to carry, Almi," he replied, when I finished. "First, I'm glad that Alan is finally coming around and can help you carry that burden with your mother. With Kane, I'm at a loss for words. I agree with you when you said that when someone loves you the way he say he does, he would have done everything he could not to hurt you. Temptation will always be around, but that does not mean he has to succumb to it. I feel like men, well some women too, make excuses to cheat on their significant other. There is absolutely no reason in the world to go to the next person when you a good man or woman at home. If they're not good to you, then leave the relationship, but don't do all that cheating stuff."

I don't know where this man had been hiding all my life, but it was very refreshing to see that there were men who felt this way and knew how to be faithful. "So you never cheated on anyone before?" I asked, raising my eyebrow.

"Never," he said with no hesitation.

"Well, good for you," I said, trying to sound nonchalant, but was actually quite impressed. I would be lying right now if I didn't wish he was my man. At least I'm pretty sure we would have been happy, and he would have been loyal to me. There was nothing wrong with a little wishful thinking.

"You're a really nice woman, Almi, and you're strong. You carry a lot of weight on your shoulders, but I admire how you still push and handle your business," he said.

This man didn't know me outside of work, but he drew that conclusion about me. "I appreciate the compliment." I blushed.

"It's the truth," he said.

Before I could say anything else, my cell phone

rang. I put my finger up to Marshall, signaling for him to give me a moment, because I wasn't finished with this conversation. My heart started racing, and I got a sinking feeling in the pit of my stomach because the call was coming from the nursing home. They should only be calling me if there was an emergency with my mother.

"H-Hello?" I answered nervously, preparing for the inevitable.

"Hello, Almi. It's Dr. Ackerman. Is now a good time to speak with you?" he asked.

"Um, yes. I have a moment," I said, still bracing for bad news. At least he didn't tell me he needed me to come to the nursing home right away. Since he didn't, that could only mean my mother was still alive for now, so I began breathing again slowly.

"As you know, we've been conducting tests for a few weeks now. I don't know how, but the CT technician may have possibly missed this before. It looks like Mrs. Prentiss has a tumor on her brain. That may be the answer to why it seems the Alzheimer's is progressing so quickly. I'm afraid that your mother has brain cancer." He broke the news to me.

"Brain cancer!" I exclaimed with tears immediately filling my eyes.

"I'm sorry, Almi. Yes, she has cancer. It appears it's already in stage three and progressing to stage four quite rapidly," he said regrettably. "There is usually no association between traumatic brain injury and cancer; however, there is a very small percentage it can be an inflammatory response, such as this one."

"You know what, Dr. Ackerman? Fuck you! Fuck that nursing home! Fuck the CT technician! This is something you all should have known a long time ago. I promise I am filing a medical malpractice lawsuit against you sorry son of a bitches!" I screamed into the phone before hanging up.

The room started spinning, and I plopped down in my chair to catch my breath. I could hear Marshall asking me if I was alright in the background, and I was so in shock right that I couldn't even answer. How the hell did these careless assholes miss a whole entire tumor? People didn't seem to care when it wasn't their loved one. This was my mother. The only mother I had. I was so distraught right now that I didn't even realize I was hyperventilating. I had already popped a pill a little while ago, so I couldn't take another one yet. I practiced deep breaths until I was calm enough to hear Marshall say he was taking me home. I didn't argue with him but just grabbed my things and followed him out the building after he locked my office up for me.

We rode in silence, with the exception of me giving him my parent's address. I wanted to head to the nursing home to be by mother's side, but I was so upset that I was bound to murder Dr. Ackerman or snap on one of the nurses, and I couldn't allow myself to do that. I just wanted to go crawl in bed long enough to process this and gather my strength before I head down there. I was so lost in my thoughts that I didn't realize we had arrived until Marshall opened my door for me. I let us in, and he sat on the couch next to me rubbing my hand.

"What's going on, Almi?" Alan said, yawning and coming down the stairs. He eyed Marshall suspiciously.

"I got a call from the doctor. Mama has brain

cancer." I could barely choke out between tears.

"She what!" he yelled out. He grabbed his jacket and keys and told me to come on.

"I can't go down there right now. I need a few moments," I replied while staring off into space.

"I know this is awkward. I'm Marshall, her co-worker. I brought Almi home when she got really distraught," Marshall said, introducing himself to my brother.

"Thank you very much, Marshall. I appreciate that. I'm her brother, Alan," he said, shaking Marshall's hand.

"Her car is still at the job. I'll leave you my telephone number if you need me to come back and get her or even take you down there to get it," he said, handing him one of his business cards.

"Yeah, we'll take care of it. I'm going to run out to the nursing home to see what's going on. Are you sure you're not coming, Almi?'

"I'm sure. I'll go down there later. I just can't right now." I shook my head, blowing out a breath.

The front door opened and closed a few minutes

later, and I wiped my face with the back of my hand. Marshall handed me a Kleenex off the coffee table and asked if I minded him going to the kitchen to get me a glass of water. I instructed him to grab me a bottled water from the fridge. He did just that and sat with me a few more moments, allowing me to cry on his shoulder before breaking the silence.

"I don't want to leave you like this, but I should probably get back to the office. Will you be alright?" he asked.

"Marshall, please don't leave me yet," I told him. "I really need you here right now."

"Then I'll stay," he replied softly.

I leaned back on him, and he pulled me closer. It felt good when I felt him kiss the top of my head and began rubbing my arm. I could stay like this with him forever. For some reason, it felt right. I don't know if it was a lapse of judgment or just my emotions speaking for me. I almost kicked myself after I said it.

"Marshall, I need you," I whispered.

"Shhh. Almi, you got me. Just rest up," he

whispered back.

That was all I needed to hear, and for some reason, I believed him. I usually wasn't some gullible or naïve female, but I think we both knew we had one hell of a connection from the first day we laid eyes on each other. I was with Kane then, so there was no way I was going to pursue anything with Marshall. Even now, it was still way too soon since my break up from Kane was still very fresh. What I knew for sure was that my friendship with Marshall was something I wouldn't be able to let go of now. He was there for me when I needed him most. He understood me in ways Kane didn't.

For a moment, I began to wonder if that's how he felt about Zavia. I didn't know if it was only about him fulfilling a sexual need or if she fulfilled him in more ways than one. A part of me wanted to be understanding because we were making so much progress, but another part of me knew I deserved way better than how he had hurt me. We invested so many years into each other that I couldn't see myself just throwing it away, but when there was a man like Marshall giving me all his attention, it made me second-guess the relationship I had with Kane.

I lifted my head off his shoulder and looked Marshall in his eyes. They were so warm and inviting. I couldn't stop myself from the temptation that was beginning to consume me. I leaned in to kiss his lips, and I was relieved that he didn't resist but kissed me back. He parted my lips with his, and our tongues began to intertwine into a perfect dance. I lost myself, and this man and all sense of myself and control of my actions went out the window. I pulled him up and had him follow me upstairs to my old bedroom where I had been sleeping.

I started kissing him again and began tugging at his pants to loosen his belt and unzip them. He pulled his face away from mine and grabbed my hands to stop me. I looked at him with pleading eyes to make love to me, and he looked back at me with understanding eyes.

"Almi, not this way. As much as I want to make love to you, I care about you too much to take advantage of you this way. You're vulnerable right now with the situation with both Kane and your mother."

"Oh my God! My mother! How could I have

forgotten that fast?" I exclaimed! I was in the middle of a nervous breakdown and was trying to avoid facing reality that I completely pushed her cancer diagnosis out of my head.

"If you want, I can go down to the nursing home with you to be there for support," he said.

God, where has this man been my entire life? I hated to continue comparing him to Kane, but he never offered to go visit my mother with me. Now that I thought about it, he wasn't really that supportive during this process at all. "Yes, I would like that." I smiled at him. At this moment, I knew there was something special between Marshall and I that I wasn't willing to let go.

Chapter 15 Kane

Almi didn't seem too interested in helping me out of this situation, so I resorted to the next best thing, and that was calling my father. I really didn't want to get him involved, but I was his son, and he had money, so there should be no issue with him posting my bail. I would do everything I could to pay him back as soon as possible if he wanted me to. I waited around for a couple more days since talking to Almi just to see if she'd change her mind and come through for me. When I saw that she was standing firm, I made up in my mind that the next time they let us out of our cells, I was heading to the phone to call my dad. I was still waiting for them to assign me my custody level, so for now, I was in reception and orientation where the calls were still free. I was glad that I had memorized his number, or I would have been screwed.

I listened as the recording went through the entire spiel about how the call would be recorded and what option for him to push to accept or reject the call. I was glad he accepted it because within a few seconds, his voice came over the phone.

"Hello?" he answered, almost hesitantly.

"Dad?" I asked shyly, making sure it was him, but also embarrassed to be calling him from jail.

"Dad?" He chuckled. "That's a first. You've never referred to me as that before. Do I even want to really know why you're calling me from jail?"

"I've been accused of rape," I said regrettably.

"I'm sorry to hear that," he said.

"I need your help," I continued.

"So now you need my help," he replied sarcastically. "Oh how the tables have turned."

I was about to hang up because I didn't have time for this. For some reason, he seemed to find my current situation amusing, but there was nothing funny about being in jail, especially for something I didn't do. I wondered why he was acting so strangely toward me all of a sudden when he was so adamant about us building a relationship. It didn't take long for me to get the answer.

"Well, Kane… it's interesting how you need me, but you couldn't be there for me when I needed you," he finally said.

I soon realized this was about that damned kidney. In no way did I ever think this would come back to bite me in the ass. It had finally dawned on me that he was using me all along. He never cared about a father-son relationship. He was spinning me until I became comfortable enough with him for him to ask me to donate. Now I felt like my back was against the wall, and I would willingly give him what he wanted if he could help me out of this.

"A kidney is a major thing to ask for, but if that's what you want, you can have it. What if I'm not a match?" I asked him.

"We'll cross that bridge later. At least get tested so you can see. How much is your bond?"

"They set it at $100,000 cash bond; however, 10% will be accepted."

"I'll come post it in a few minutes, just in time for you to attend this doctor appointment with me."

I was not happy about this at all, but I guess $10,000 wasn't a bad price for a kidney. I just hoped I wouldn't need it later in life one day. I also knew I would never be able to look at my father the same way after this. He was never there for me, and if one really looked at it, he owed me. Too bad he didn't see it that way but was looking to gain something from all of this. In the end, it was going to be a win-win situation for both of us. I hung up the phone relieved that I would soon be walking out these doors. I had one more favor to ask him once he arrived. I didn't want to use a public defender and wanted him to foot the bill for a lawyer as well.

Chapter 16 Almi

I hollered out as Marshall dug deeper, touching my very soul with his male organ. He was taking me on the ride of my life right now, and I promised that not even sex with Kane had ever felt better. Marshall had skills, and he took me to levels I had never been on before. I was almost afraid to open my eyes because I was hoping this moment wasn't just a dream. With another deep thrust, I knew this was real, and my juices oozed down his shaft as he brought another orgasm out of me. I was spent, and he knew it, so he sped up, releasing his own nut only a few seconds later.

Marshall and I had been spending a lot of time together these past few days. He was nothing but a gentleman and was in no rush to have sex. I have to admit that I couldn't help myself and came on to him once again. This time he didn't stop me, and I'm glad he didn't, because now I felt like I had received a piece of heaven with him. Besides sex, he was very supportive of what I was going through and always went with me to see my mother. He was a lot of fun to hang out with as well, and I couldn't believe I had been missing out on so much fun by playing a housewife to Kane. I would be lying if I was to say I didn't miss him, but besides my mother being ill, things were going a little better in my life.

So far as my mother, I was still considering filing a lawsuit. The doctor and all the specialists have been very apologetic for not catching her cancer sooner, but I still felt there were no excuses. She had gone through a couple of rounds of treatments these past few days and was out of the hospital and back at the nursing home. My head was still all over the place with this situation, but at this point, all I could do was be there for my mother. I was glad that Alan had finally stepped up and was able to help me bear this heavy burden. He had finally gone back home to his woman, but he was still very active in checking on our mother and seeing how things were going. Now that I understood why he avoided her the way he did, I couldn't hold it against him any longer. That was the past, and since he was more available in the present, I figured that was all that mattered at this point.

It felt good to be cuddled close to Marshall, but I pulled away from him so I could roll over and face him. I kissed his lips, and when he smiled, it warmed my heart. Never in a million years did I think I would be lying here with him. I was so determined to remain loyal to my relationship with Kane, despite my attraction to this man lying right here before me. I mean, technically, I *was* loyal to him. I never cheated, but there was still a part of me that felt weird about it. I sometimes kicked myself for crossing that line with a co-worker because we all knew the old saying that it wasn't good to mix business with pleasure, but since I wasn't his boss and he wasn't mine, none of that really mattered.

"What's on your mind, beautiful?" he asked.

"You really want to know?" I raised my eyebrow.

"If I didn't I wouldn't have asked," he replied.

"I'm was just hoping that we wouldn't regret crossing that line, considering we work together. I wouldn't want for things not to work out with us and it create workplace tension."

"I'm not worried about that at all. I believe our friendship is quite genuine, so whatever path we go on, I think we'll be fine. I understand you still have some healing to do from your relationship with Kane, so I'm in no rush to pressure you to make us official. You're free do whatever and with whomever, but I would definitely like for things to progress with us."

I melted at his words. He always seemed to know what to say. "I would like for things to go further with us as well. I definitely need some time to make sure I'm over him before I pursue anything with you. As far as anyone else, there is no one else. Just you," I assured him.

"Well, that's nice to know," he said, kissing me again.

"I don't know if I should be offended or not that you thought there was." I playfully nudged him.

"Please don't be. We're adults, and I know that sometimes a woman has needs," he said.

"Well, why don't you fulfill this need throbbing between my legs," I said sexily.

"Oh, so you're ready for round two now?" He chuckled.

I bit my bottom lip in response. He licked his and pulled me on top of him. I slid my wet pussy right down onto him and began to ride him slowly as he massaged my nipples. I threw my head back and let out a deep moan as I enjoyed the electrifying shocks that soared through my body. I don't know if it was too soon to say this, but I wanted to be in this moment with Marshall forever. I felt like I needed to be here with him forever. Hell, I loved this man.

***

The next morning at work in the break room, Winnie cut her eyes at us as Marshall and I stood close to each other and shared a laugh. I was getting sick of her ass by the day, but as long as she stayed in her place and kept her mouth shut, there was nothing I could do about the way she looked at me. I saw her roll her eyes, so I stood on my tippy toes to give Marshall a kiss just to push her buttons a little more.

Winnie cleared her throat. "If you care at all to know, Almi, my father bonded Kane out the other day, and he's been staying at my father's place. You might wanna check on *your man* and see how he's holding up," she said.

I guess she thought she was really doing something

by saying that, as if Marshall already didn't know about Kane. Besides, he wasn't my man anymore, so I didn't give two shits about how he was doing. "Maybe you didn't get the memo, but Kane and I broke up." I shrugged.

"Humph," was her reply as she tossed her hair back and walked out of the break room.

"What is her problem?" Marshall asked like he really didn't know.

"Don't stand there and act like you didn't know that girl wants you and wants you bad." I chuckled.

"Nah, I really didn't know. I always thought she was a bit overly friendly, but I didn't think anything of it."

"Are you serious? So you *never* noticed her flirting with you?"

"I really didn't. I've been so busy watching you and trying to control my attraction and desire for you that I never paid her or anyone else any mind."

He made me blush, so I turned away. I rubbed the nape of my neck and bit my bottom lip. "I will see you after work." I quickly kissed him on the cheek and switched out of the break room to my office.

"You know what you're doing, Almi, is pathetic," Winnie called out as I walked past her office.

I stopped dead in my tracks and took a few steps backward to her door. "Excuse me?" I scrunched up my face confusedly. I knew damn well her ass wasn't talking to me.

"It's not a good look on you the way you throw yourself all over that man," she said disgustedly.

"Is that not the same thing you were doing? By the way, let me correct you. I never *threw* myself at that man. If you must know, he was digging me this whole time, but I was too busy trying to be a good woman to your no-good brother."

"I'm just calling it how I see it." She shook her head.

"I don't give a damn what you see or what it is you think you're speaking on, but I really think you should mind your business. You being all up in mine is most certainly not a classy look for you. Now I can stand here and go back and forth with you all day and be catty, but I have more important things to do. Just keep in mind that

I'm from the hood, and I can get down like bitch in the hood, so don't let the workplace demeanor fool you, boo. Good day, ma'am." I gave her a fake smile, and walked away.

I heard her mumble the word bitch under her breath, but I wasn't going to give her the satisfaction of reacting to it. I was a careerwoman first, and I'd be damned if I let some low-life slut take me out of character and make me lose my job. I was unapologetically me, and it wasn't my problem that she couldn't handle it.

The workday went by rather quickly, and I was a little disappointed when Marshall said he couldn't hang out with me tonight because he was hanging out with the fellas instead. I swear I needed some friends, but I kind of enjoyed being a loner. I had never really been one to hang out with other females for real. Every once in a while, I'd envy friendships, like the ones in the movie *Girl's Trip*, but for the most part, I felt like my life was more peaceful by keeping to myself. Besides, I was always busy working, dating Kane, and looking after my mother. I honestly didn't have time for a social life outside of that.

Since I no longer had plans with Marshall for the evening, I figured I would go ahead and visit my mother after work and then head on home to get some rest. As much as I liked being at my parents' house, because it would always be home, it was just way too big and lonely right now. I was really thinking about looking for another place now and discussing with Alan the possibility of going forward with selling the house. I was totally against it at first, but now, it only seemed like the right thing to do. I would have loved to have children one day and they grow up here like I did, but that house held so many memories that centered around the pain I felt at this moment.

When I pulled in my usual parking spot at the nursing home, I exhaled deeply. Sooner than later, I was going to have to face my reality and accept my mother's fate. No one was ready to lose their mother, and it was hard as hell knowing that nine times out of ten, she wasn't going to make it because the cancer was eating away at her. I was a firm believer that God had the final say so, but people had to understand that is exactly what it means. God's final say so may be to give His children sweet rest and call them on home. Our selfish reasons for wanting to hold people here could totally be against God's plans. We each have a day of birth and a day of death, and that's just how life goes. I took another deep breath, popped a pill, and took a huge sip of water before getting out of my car. My panic attacks seemed to be under control, but they were easily triggered whenever I became upset. I had no idea how this visit was going to go, so I wanted to be prepared for whatever may come my way.

I promise my intuition must have kicked in full speed, because as soon as I made it to my mother's room, I definitely was not prepared for what I saw. Kane was sitting by my mother's bedside, stroking her hand, and speaking gently to her. I stood in the doorway for a minute, since his back was turned to me, and listened to everything he told her. Her eyes were closed, and lately, she seemed to not be responding to much of anything, so I wasn't even sure if she was really taking in what he was saying.

"I know I haven't been the best to Almi, and I should have been better to you by being here, but I'm here now. I want you to forgive me for my absence and forgive me for hurting your daughter. Although I never got to know you during the days you were well, you still knew who I was, nonetheless, when you met me, and you trusted me with your most precious jewel, your daughter. Almi means everything to me. If she were to ever give me another chance, I promise you and her that I will do right by her. She's a good woman, and she deserves better than the way I hurt her. I was weak and selfish, but I really did learn my lesson. I don't know which way your health is going to turn, but I pray for you every day. I hope you pull through this," he said, kissing her hand.

I smiled and quickly wiped my falling tears away. It was nice that he finally made his way down here, and I could hear the sincerity in his voice. I believed he was being completely genuine in this moment, and it pulled at my heartstrings. I didn't want to be weak for this man, but I really did miss him. I was excited about the new adventure I had embarked on with Marshall, but I'd be lying to myself if I said I was over Kane or wasn't still in love with him. I didn't know what our future would hold or if I would ever get past the hurt he put me through, but after hearing him just now, I felt like the least bit I could do was try. I was probably being stupid, but then again, maybe I wasn't. I would never know if life could have been better for us if I didn't at least try.

I cleared my throat before I spoke. "That was very sweet what you just said, Kane. Thank you for coming down here to see her. That means a lot to me, and I'm sure it would mean a whole lot to her." I smiled weakly.

"Almi!" he exclaimed excitedly. "Baby, I am so sorry. I promise to God I am. Please, please forgive me, baby. I know you may still need some time, and that's OK. Take as much time as you need. I just want you to know that I promise to God I didn't rape that girl. What I told you was true about only being with her once, but that was at her will, not forced. I'm telling the truth when I say she let herself into our home that night with the spare key. She was only trying to trap me because she was mad I called things off. I will never do anything to hurt you again if you just give me another chance," he begged.

"Kane," I whispered. "I know you didn't rape that girl. In my heart, I know you didn't. I tossed it over in my head so many times, and I was hurt, so there was a small part of me that wondered if you did. I know you though, and I know your character. You wouldn't force someone to have sex with you. I just know you wouldn't," I replied.

"Thank you for finally believing me, bae. Again, take all the time you need to gather your thoughts, but please come home once you've had more time to calm down. I want us to work things out," he said.

I walked up to him, gave him a hug, and very passionate kiss. I told him right now was not the time to finish this conversation, but we'd finish talking once we left here. I pulled away from him and took a seat in the chair where he was just sitting. I leaned forward to kiss my mother's forehead and began stroking her hand. I told her about my day and let her know I loved her very much. She continued to lie there with her eyes clothes and looked as peaceful as ever.

When we finished our visit, I asked Kane to come back to my parents' home with me, and he obliged. I wasn't ready to head back to our house yet, but I did want him to spend the night with me. We made love like never before, and it felt good to be back in his arms when we cuddled. I didn't know how I was going to tell Marshall that I was getting back with Kane. I also hoped this wouldn't be a decision that I'd later regret, but only time would tell.

Chapter 17 Kane

I couldn't believe that my father had convinced me to give him a kidney, all because I needed him. He was a very wealthy man and could have gotten a kidney from anyone. I guess it was easier to target me because being his son, I was likely to be a match. Needless to say, I was disappointed as hell when he turned out to be right after I was tested. Now here I was, lying in my hospital bed, preparing for surgery to have my kidney removed so he could get another chance at life. I guess we could call it even though because he was giving me another chance at life as well. Not only did he bail me out, but he also hired me one of the best attorneys in St. Louis, Scott Hefty. He had a proven track record for winning all his criminal cases or striking some damn good plea deals, so I knew I was in good hands.

Almi wasn't that excited about what I was doing and said she always felt like something was a bit shady about my father from the day she met him. She also brought me up to speed about how childish Winnie was in the workplace as well and gave me heads-up on some things she may try to tell me about some guy named Marshall. Although it did hurt to know that Almi had begun moving on, I couldn't be mad because of how I did her. I was just happy she forgave me, and we both just needed to put the past behind us at this point. The reality was, I had already heard about this Marshall guy that one night Winnie called and said she needed to holler at me about Almi. I never got to ask her about it because when she came home she confronted me about Zavia. The only thing that wasn't clear to me was whether Almi was messing around with him before or after she found out about old girl. Winnie made it seem like it was before, but Almi clearly said it was after. Either way it went, the past was going to have to stay in the past.

  Although Almi was not 100% supportive of what I was doing, she was here by my side at this moment and promised me she'd be at my side whenever I woke up from surgery. I was beyond grateful for this woman and was going to do everything I could to make up for all my wrongdoings. I made small talk with Almi while I waited to be taken down to the operating room. The anesthesiologist already left my room giving me his speech, and the doctor came in right after him to give me his spiel. I was just ready to get this over with and move forward. I prayed to God that if my other kidney failed me one day, someone would be willing to give me one. Meanwhile, as soon as I recovered from surgery, I made up in my mind that it was time to propose to Almi and make her my wife as soon as possible.

***

It had been a little over a month since the procedure, and I had healed pretty well. My father told me he was doing pretty good as well and thanked me several times for giving him my kidney. I was still feeling salty about how everything went down, but everything was over and done with now. On the other hand, life still wasn't what I thought it would be. I was terminated from the college and having a hard time finding another job. Getting fired from my last two jobs was not helping my employment record at all. I was to the point that I figured working a dead-end job was going to be my only option, and I had to do something fast to keep from backtracking to that place I was a few months ago when Almi had to hold things down. She gave me another chance, and I didn't want her to change her mind and leave me.

I was doing everything I could to be attentive to her. I went with her to visit her mother, and I sexed her up pretty good. Eventually, all of this would get old and probably wouldn't be enough to keep her happy if I couldn't do my part to provide for her or at least share in the load of maintaining our household. I held off a little longer on asking her to marry me, because right now, I wasn't in a position to be husband material to her. I felt like I was still losing this battle, and I needed to figure out how to get on my A-game and fast.

I considered asking my father for more money but thought against it. Perry said he could get me a job with is company, but I'd have to be willing to relocate to Chicago. I already knew that wasn't an option because Almi wasn't going to want to move there, even though I knew there were a million accounting jobs there. I just figured I had to do what I had to do, swallow my pride, and take whatever job I could get. With that in mind, I took a deep breath as

I climbed out my car and walked with my head held high into the Dollar Tree. I was interviewing for a management position, and since I needed this job more than ever, I had to get in here and do my thing.

Apparently, I did just that because I walked out of there with an immediate job offer. I was scheduled for orientation the following week and was happy about having job security again. It wasn't the best job, but it was a job, and that's all that mattered. I knew Almi would be proud of me, and I wanted us to celebrate. I stopped at Schnucks Grocery Store on my way home, grabbed some of her favorite wine, corn on the cob to make, a container of coleslaw, and had them fry up some catfish at the hot-food counter. I figured I might as well grab a box of the Red Lobster biscuit mix and a cheesecake from the freezer for dessert as well. I was excited to get home and prepare dinner for my queen.

On my way home, I stopped at the bank so I could grab my grandmother's wedding ring out of my safe-deposit box. I already had it sized and cleaned, so I knew it was the perfect fit for Almi. I didn't want to waste any more days being her boyfriend. I was ready to make this woman my wife. She had stuck by my side for better or for worse, and she has only made my life better day by day. I couldn't see myself without this woman, and I figured now was as good of a time as any to make us officially husband and wife.

Almi walked in right as I took the biscuits out the oven. Dinner was ready, and I couldn't wait to not only share my good news about getting another job today, but I was anxious to propose to her. When she smiled and it lit up the room, I knew in my heart I was making the right decision this evening.

"How was your day?" she asked as she placed her briefcase on the counter and kissed me.

"It was a good day," I told her, trying to sound as nonchalant as possible. I wasn't ready to give anything away yet since I was still setting the mood. I wanted this moment to be perfect.

"Are you ready to eat now, or did you want to get comfortable first?" I asked her.

"It's been a long day, and I'm going to take a quick

shower while you finish up in here," she said.

I already knew that was going to be her answer, so I was ten steps ahead of her. I already had some of her sexy lingerie laid out on the bed with rose petals that led from our bedroom to her bubble bath. We had already had this conversation about baths a few times before, but I knew she wouldn't complain and just enjoy the moment. My assumptions were confirmed when I heard her squeal and yell out the room how sweet all of this was. I poured her a glass of wine and took it to the bathroom as she lowered herself into the tub.

"I love you so much, Almi," I told her. Her beauty was breathtakingly amazing, and after all these years, it still mesmerized me.

"I love you too, Kane." She smiled.

We made small talk as she leaned back and relaxed. I wanted every day to be perfect like this. I *needed* for everyday to be perfect like this. When she finished with her bath, I helped her step out the tub, handing a towel and her robe. I told her I was heading to the kitchen to make our plates while she went on to the bedroom to lotion up and slide into her teddy. Call me old fashioned for still liking lingerie and wanting to pamper my woman, but I was willing to do anything to make her feel special. I also thought it was sexy as hell that she would sit at the kitchen table and have dinner with in her lingerie.

Midway through dinner, I went ahead and told her about getting a job. She was genuinely happy for me and didn't judge me in any way. That was one thing I really loved about this woman. She was just happy that I was working. She didn't care where. She never made me feel bad for having to downgrade a little but was very supportive regardless. I was overwhelmed with so much love for this woman that it was nothing for me to pull the ring from my pocket and drop down on one knee before her.

"Almi, will you marry me?"

Chapter 18 Almi

Kane did a complete turnaround on me, and it was so sudden that I wasn't sure if I trusted it. As wonderful as he was being to me, I didn't know who this man was anymore. I would be lying if I said I didn't regret taking him back. Why couldn't he be this good to me in the beginning before he messed up? I was so conflicted because now I was living a double life. I couldn't let Marshall go like I thought I would be able to. He gave me this different perspective on life, and I really enjoyed being with him. I told Marshall I was considering getting back with Kane without being forward and telling him that I already had. I figured he pretty much knew the obvious because I wasn't hanging out as much. We did play hooky from work the other day though and spent an entire day making love for hours at my parents' home. I didn't know what the hell to do at this point because I was torn between two men.

It's crazy, because for a minute, it seemed that Kane was the stranger in our house, but now, it was me. He had no idea of the things I did behind his back, and I knew he would be beyond hurt if he were to find out. I had to figure out what to do and fast, especially since I had accepted his proposal. I was in utter shock that he finally popped the question that I didn't think the situation through but immediately said yes. It definitely wasn't the proposal I had hoped for all these years, but I guess it was better than none.

I had always dreamed of a lot of people being around, whether it was him proposing to me in front of family and friends or him doing it in public and strangers would cheer us on once I said yes. It seemed so spur of the moment, and I wasn't thrilled about it being in the privacy of our home, but I was still glad he had finally done it. I guess that was his way of letting me know he was serious about correcting his faults, especially since he gave me his grandmother's wedding ring. That alone let me know I had to get a grip on myself and figure out who I wanted to be with.

Kane and I were on our way to the nursing home to visit my mother. Alan said he would meet us there as usual. While Kane drove, I texted back and forth with Marshall, who had a huge smile on my face. I saw Kane look at me sideways a couple of times, but he didn't press the issue. I knew I would come up with some lie if he were to ask me what was up, because I had already gotten good at it lately. There was a small part of me that felt bad because two wrongs didn't make a right, and I had drug poor Marshall into this love triangle, but another part of me wanted revenge deep down. If Kane was to find out that I was still messing around with Marshall, there was a piece of me that would get a lot of satisfaction from him hurting like he had hurt me.

When we arrived at the nursing home, Alan met us at the door. I could tell the entire mood at the place was solemn, and the expression on Alan's face said it all. I was preparing to hear the inevitable, and my stomach began doing flip flops. Tears had already formed in my eyes. I just knew he was about to tell me our mother had passed away; however, he didn't. What he said was no better, because it still meant the same thing. The doctor had told him that he cancer had attacked very aggressively, and he was giving her a couple more weeks at most to live. He told me it was time to begin making funeral arrangements.

I can't tell you what else happened after that. I just know that I found myself wandering down Broadway near Interstate 55 when I snapped back to reality as I noticed nightfall was upon me. I know when I ran out of the nursing home, I heard both Kane and Alan call after me, but neither of them gave chase. I guess they figured I needed some time to myself. I don't even know exactly how much time I had to myself because everything that took place after that was a blur. I was so lost in my thoughts that I literally just came back to reality a few minutes ago.

I grabbed my phone from my pocket and saw that both Kane and Alan had been trying to reach me endlessly. I still wasn't ready to talk to them. It's crazy because I didn't want anyone but Marshall at this moment. I felt like he was the only person who could make things better for me right now. Right as I was about to call him, my phone rang with a call from Kane. I was about to answer it but pushed ignore and proceeded to call Marshall. He answered on the first ring, and I asked him to pick me up from the service station right near Broadway and Osceola.

I was nervous as hell because there was a bunch of dope fiends walking around, but I was tired of walking and couldn't take another step. While I waited for him, Kane text me asking where I was and said he was worried. He claimed he drove all over town looking for me. I rolled my eyes and just wanted him to leave me alone at the moment.

Marshall pulled up, and I got up off the curb I was sitting on to climb into his car. He leaned over to push the door open for me, and I smiled when I saw him. He smiled back softly and leaned over to kiss the top of my head once I sank into the soft leather seats of his car. I blew out a breath and shook my head. I was still trying to make sense of my life because at this moment I was so lost. I hated that things had to be this way.

"What happened?" he finally asked, as we went south on Interstate 55.

"They gave my mother about two weeks to live," I whispered.

"I'm sorry, baby," he said, stroking my hand.

"Thank you for picking me up," I told him.

"How'd you end up here?" he inquired.

"I ran off from the nursing home when I got the news, and I guess this is just where I ended up." I shrugged.

"You walked all the way over here from Grand and Magnolia!" he exclaimed.

"I guess so," I said.

"Do you want me to take you back to the nursing home to get your car?" he asked.

"I didn't park at the nursing home," I said quietly.

He didn't say anything but continued to look straight ahead as he drove. He was acting a little weird all of a sudden, but my mind was so far gone that I didn't even want to figure out what his issue was this evening. For now, I just enjoyed the peace and quiet while I rested my aching feet.

"What's going on with you and Kane?" he asked out of nowhere.

"Where the hell did that come from?" I asked defensively.

"It's just a question. I want to know where things stand with you two and where things are going with us?"

"There's nothing going on with me and Kane." I

lied. "You and I are still progressing, aren't we?" I asked, looking at him.

"That's what I thought. I guess I was wrong though," he said.

My heart started racing because he was talking in circles instead of just coming right out to say what was on his mind. "You're not wrong."

"I'm not?" he asked, raising his eyebrow.

"I mean… look, I'm just tired, so I can't even comprehend what I'm trying to say right now. We're fine, Marshall. Everything is fine with us," I tried to assure him.

"Well, if that's the case, why are you sporting a huge ass wedding ring on your finger?" he asked.

I sighed and wanted to kick myself. I had gotten so good about sliding it off my finger when I knew I was going to be in Marshall's presence, and this time I forgot to. Damn. I took a deep breath before I spoke. "He proposed," I said quietly.

"I can see that, and I can also see you accepted," he said matter-of-factly.

"It was so spur of the moment, and with so much

going on, I just said yes. I've had a lot of time to think about things though, and I want to be with you Marshall," I told him sincerely, taking the ring off my finger.

"No, put it back on," he said. "You obviously made your decision. Keep that same energy you had when you accepted the proposal and be with him," he said.

He had gotten off the highway at the Lindbergh Blvd exit and was heading to Tesson Ferry Road, toward my parents' house to drop me off.

"Are you really going to do this now?" I asked him.

"Almi, I like you a whole lot. I care deeply about you. Hell, I love you. However, you still have feelings for him, and I can't come between that. I've been patient with you, and I never pursued you while you were with him because I respected what you two had. When my chance finally came, I was hesitant but went in full force. I don't regret it at all because we've spent so many moments together that I'll forever cherish. The reality is, you belong to another man, and I think the best thing for me to do is just fall back," he said. I could tell he was hurt. I hated things had to come to this because I was more than certain

I was going to choose him. I just needed a little more time. Unfortunately, I was out of time, and Marshall had made that decision for me. For us.

He was a complete gentleman and walked me to the door of my parents' home. He kissed me deeply before he walked way, and I couldn't stop the tears from flowing. As much as I loved Kane, I felt I really knew love when I was with Marshall. He was perfect for me in every way, but now I had lost him. I went into my parents' house and laid down in my bed. I was awakened up by Alan and Kane when they burst into the room. They were both going in because I had been ignoring them, and they were worried. I just rolled over and tried to go back to sleep. Kane got it the bed with me and pulled me close. I had to admit that it did feel good to be in his arms, so I snuggled closer to him. It looked like this was going to be my life, so I might as well embrace it.

Chapter 19 Kane

Almi had been acting rather strangely, but I chalked it up to her mourning over the news about her mother. Two weeks had come and gone, and she was still holding on for dear life. Almi and Alan had already gone ahead and made funeral arrangements for their mother. I felt horribly for her and what she was going through. I wanted to do everything I could to make things better for her, but she was so withdrawn and didn't seem to want to be bothered. I even saw that she didn't have her ring on the night me and Alan found her at their parents' house. With everything going on, I didn't want to question her about it, but I found that to be a little weird. She had put it back on since then, but she was still acting like she didn't want to be with me or around me. Maybe I was thinking too hard about things, and I just needed to allow her some space while she processed this situation with her mother. Something else was telling me that it was much deeper though.

I wanted to do what I could to cheer her up, so I had organized a surprise engagement party for her to officially announce or engagement and celebrate with our family and friends. Almi didn't really have too many friends, but I did invite some of our friends from college, and even my mother and Perry were coming into town tonight for this event. My mother hadn't been to St. Louis since she left over thirty years ago, so tonight was going to be very special.

    I convinced Almi to go pamper herself by getting her nails and hair done. She argued me up and down but finally obliged, and she was out handling that now. Winnie wasn't too happy about it, but she helped me pick out a nice evening gown for Almi to wear. Surprisingly, she picked something very nice, considering I knew they didn't really care much for each other.

    As I got myself ready, my phone rang, pulling me from the groove I was in. I was going to ignore it so I could stay focused, but I saw that it was my father. He was expected to be in attendance as well, and I wanted to answer it in case his call was relevant to tonight. He had paid for the hall where we were having the party and even took care of the DJ and catering.

"Hello?" I answered.

"Kane, I need a minute of your time. Scott Hefty has been trying to reach you—" He started to say, but I cut him off.

"I was over here trying to get ready. My phone has been ringing every few minutes, and if I kept taking calls, I wasn't going to make it out of here on time," I told him, wanting to rush him along and off the phone as well.

"Your case has taken an amazing turn and the charges have been dropped," my father told. me.

"Huh?" I asked, confused but happy, nonetheless. "How? What happened?"

"That young lady Zavia was found dead in her apartment this morning by one of her relatives. She left a suicide note explaining everything. It's unfortunate that she really struggled with some serious mental health issues, but it worked in your favor," he said.

I breathed a sigh of relief. Although Zavia took me through hell, I still hated to hear that she took her own life. Sometimes you never knew what a person was going through and what was behind the smile they displayed. I never knew she had any issues because she seemed so happy all the time and very well put together, but I guess this was just proof that you never really knew. I was just glad that this part of my life was over, and I could finally begin moving forward. I was ready to live the rest of my life with Almi, and the very person who threatened our relationship was no longer a factor.

I hung up the phone, feeling excited about celebrating with my love and all the people who mattered to us tonight. I felt like this was a huge step in the right direction, and I was feeling pretty confident that things were going to be OK between us going forward. I took a deep breath and smiled when I heard Almi come through the door. I had her dress and Christian Dior stilettos lying out on the bed. When she came in, she looked surprised and smiled.

"To what do I owe the pleasure?" she asked, gesturing toward her evening attire.

"Will you be accompanying me this evening to our engagement party?" I asked her.

Her smile lit up the room, and I was glad that this

was making her happy. She deserved the world and all the happiness life could afford. Even if for a little while, I wanted to take her mind off everything that was going on and make tonight all about her.

She went to take a shower and told me to give her a few minutes to get dressed. I went and sat on the living room sofa while I waited for her to get herself together. I text Winnie right quick to make sure everything was in order like I expected. She assured me things were just the way I asked and that our guests had already started to arrive. I was going to propose to her again in front of everyone because I know that was something she always wanted. Some may think it was silly, but I was all about making my baby's dreams come true. When she stepped into the living room, she took my breath away. Couldn't nobody tell my me that my plus-sized beauty wasn't everything, because she was.

"You ready, my queen?" I asked her.

"I'm as ready as I'll ever be," she replied softly. Something still seemed a little off, and I couldn't quite put my finger on it, but I didn't want to ruin this evening, so I left well enough alone for now.

I took her hand into mine and led her into the car, where I helped her in. I tossed my tuxedo jacket on the back seat and went around to my side of the car so we could be on our way. I put on R. L. "Good Man" and sang along to it while we rode, and I held her hand. I stole a couple of glances at her. The first time, she seemed deep in thought, staring out the window. The second time, I squeezed her hand to get her attention, and she looked at me with a smile. That's all I needed to see was her million-dollar smile that I loved so much.

Upon arrival to the hall where our party was being held, I suddenly got the jitters. I don't know why, but I was little nervous about proposing again in front of everyone. I mean, it's not like people didn't already knew we were engaged, I just guess the idea of all eyes on me made me a little nervous. Almi still seemed a little off, but she was going with the flow and was acting pleasant.

"You ready?" I asked her, as I held the front door open for her.

"Why do you keep asking me that?" She giggled.

"We're here now."

"I meant are you ready to celebrate and be the center of attention of our family and friends?" I reiterated.

"This was all sprung on me about an hour ago, but I'm here in the moment with you, so I that's what matters." She shrugged.

"I love you, Almi," I told her as we walked in and everyone started cheering and clapping. I leaned in for a kiss, and she almost reluctantly returned it. I was a little hurt, but I didn't let her or anyone else see that the way she almost curved me got to me.

"I love you too," she replied.

We went over to several people to greet them as they congratulated us, and I led her out to the dance floor. The DJ began playing Charlie Wilson "You Are", and we swayed away. I felt so in love with this woman and was happy that she was all mine. I looked into her eyes, but she seemed to be occupied by something she saw over my shoulder. Whatever it was, I could tell she wasn't pleased. I followed her stares and shrugged when I saw my sister Winnie slow dancing with some guy. I knew they didn't care for each other, but I didn't want Almi to let my sister's presence to bother her the way that it had.

"What's wrong?" I whispered.

"N-Nothing wrong," she stuttered and looked at me, forcing a smile.

I didn't believe her. "Are you sure? You seem disturbed by Winnie and that gentleman she's over there with," I said.

"I said I'm fine, Marshall!" She pulled away from me and stormed off.

I looked around embarrassed, hoping no one had heard us or noticed her reaction. The only ones who seemed to be paying attention to us were Winnie and the guy she was with. The craziest thing was that she had just called me another man's name. As much as it hurt and I knew it was something we would have to address later, right now was not the time and the place, and I had to continue to go with the flow of things.

"Hey, bro," Winnie said, coming over, leaning in, and giving me a kiss on the cheek.

"What's up, sis," I replied.

"Kane, this is my date, Marshall. Marshall, this is my brother and Almi's fiancé, Kane. Marshall is the young man who works with us," she said, letting me know this is the guy she was telling me about that day.

"Nice to meet you," I said, sucking my teeth.

He stuck his hand out to shake mine, but I just looked at it. He shook his head, chuckled, and excused himself.

"What were you thinking bringing him here tonight?" I asked Winnie in disbelief.

"I didn't think anything would be wrong with it. He's my date and our co-worker. There are a few of our other co-workers here, and I figured it would only be right to invite him too since most of the accounting firm is here," she said.

"I don't know what type of game you're playing, Winnie, but it's not funny. It's childish, and you're not about to stir up no shit," I told her, looking around to see where Almi went.

"I wasn't trying to start anything. I can't believe that you'd accuse me of that," she said innocently.

"You know… just forget it," I said, waving her off and walking away. I went to look for Almi, and when I stumbled upon her in the hallway, my heart dropped. What pissed me off was that she didn't have a care in the world because she so openly betrayed me. Her and Marshall was in the corner near the bathrooms kissing. I guess that was the reason she acted so distant toward me. She had never gotten over the feelings she developed for him. I was hurt, but I couldn't be mad. I made my bed, and I had to lie in it. A part of me wanted to act an ass and make a scene, especially since my father had paid for this party. Another part of me said I'd just let her have her moment. I don't know what made me act so maturely, but I did. I've heard the saying that sometimes you love a person enough to let them go. I had put her through so much hurt with Zavia that she found comfort in another man. I loved her enough to let her go and let her be happy.

__Epilogue__

I thought I would get pleasure in hurting Kane the way he had hurt me, but I didn't. When I finally looked up after pulling away from Marshall, I saw Kane standing there with tears in his eyes. All I could do was mouth the words, *I'm sorry,* as Marshall and I walked off. However, I am happy about the decision I made to choose Marshall.

See, Marshall was upset with me that evening after he learned that Kane and I was engaged. We still remained friends, still had lunch together, and hung out a couple more times after work. We kept everything respectful, without crossing that line again. It was hard, but I was honored that he had respect for me and my engagement. Some would still probably say if he respected it, we wouldn't have hung out, but why lose a good friend?

When I saw Marshall with Winnie at the engagement party, my heart became so overwhelmed with love for him, and I knew I couldn't fight my feelings any longer. This man was perfect for me, and I had fallen in love with him. Don't get me wrong, I loved Kane, but I wasn't in love with him. Now that I think about it, I don't think I ever was. Our relationship was merely one of convenience because we had been friends first. Usually in situations like that, it seemed like people were destined to be together, but obviously, not in our case.

It was crazy because after so many years, I thought I really knew Kane just to find out that I didn't. His act of infidelity alone showed me another side of him that I really didn't know. I also thought we had such a good friendship and relationship that he would have been more supportive of me with the situation with my mother, but he wasn't. It wasn't until later when he wanted to begin proving himself that he stepped up. Well, that's fake and that's not what I need in my life.

Meanwhile, I knew Kane would be alright. It was unfortunate what happened to Zavia, but at least he was cleared of a crime he didn't commit. He just needed time to find himself and work through all the issues he had going on with finding job stability and possibly the woman who would complete him. He often said that was me, but I believe he only felt that way once he thought he was going to lose me. People were entitled to making mistakes, but cheating was just something that blew me away, especially after all the years put into our relationship. I was over what he had done to me, and I was over him. He decided to go ahead and move to Chicago with Perry and start over fresh there. I, on the other hand, decided to hold off on selling my parents' home because I just may be willing to raise a family there one day.

My mother actually lived for three more months beyond the time the doctors gave her. Marshall squeezed my hand and kissed my cheek when the soloist at my mother's funeral began singing "One Sweet Day". I couldn't stop the tears from falling, and I would miss my mother dearly. I regretted the times I acted as if she were bothering me, but if she were still here and in her right mind, I know she would tell me not to worry about it. It was a huge responsibility and overwhelming catering to a sick parent, but I loved her dearly. I wished things had been different, and she would have never gotten into that car accident that day, but unfortunately, we don't necessarily get to choose our fate.

"I love you, Almi," Marshall said as we left the

church to get into the limo and head to her burial.

"I love you too, Marshall," I told him, meaning every word I just told him.

Marshall was sincere from day one, and he really grew on me. He had my heart. This complete stranger, who walked into my life one day at work, became the man I now felt I couldn't live without, and I knew he felt the same way about me. I felt like I owed it to us to give us a chance, and I was glad I had followed my heart. I was no longer a stranger to myself because going forward I was going to be true to myself.

The End

Be sure to LIKE our Major Key Publishing page on Facebook!